"You have n... Let me go." Yet she'd stopped struggling, merely stood straighter and unyielding in his embrace.

"No right?" He swiped his thumb across her mouth, tugging at her lower lip, feeling its luscious pad and the moist heat of her breath against his skin. Her mouth opened and those eyelids flickered betrayingly. "You give me the right when you respond to me that way." Again he slid his thumb along her mouth, this time pressing deeper, till he felt her tongue slick against his finger.

Madonna mia! How potent was this woman that the mere touch of her tongue could splinter his control?

Surprise darkened her eyes. She felt it, too.

An image filled his brain. Of rich dark hair spread over plump white pillows. Of his hands threading through its satiny splendor, splaying it out like a radiant sunburst.

Not just an image.

A memory!

D1048906

ANNIE WEST discovered romance early—her childhood best friend's house was an unending store of Harlequin® books—and she's been addicted ever since. Fortunately she found her own real-life romantic hero while studying at university, and married him. After gaining (despite the distraction) an honors classics degree, Annie took a job in the public service. For years she wrote and redrafted and revised: government plans, letters for cabinet ministers and reports for parliament. Checking the text of a novel is so much more fun!

Annie started to write romance when she took leave to spend time with her children. Between school activities she produced her first novel. At the same time she discovered Romance Writers of Australia. Since then she's been active in RWAus writers' groups and competitions. She attends annual conferences, and loves the support she gets from so many other writers. Her first Harlequin novel came out in 2005.

Annie lives with her hero (still the same one) and her children at Lake Macquarie, north of Sydney, and spends her time fantasizing about gorgeous men and their love lives. It's hard work, but she has no regrets!

Annie loves to hear from readers. You can contact her via her Web site, www.annie-west.com or at annie@annie-west.com.

FORGOTTEN MISTRESS, SECRET LOVE-CHILD
ANNIE WEST

~ REGALLY WED ~

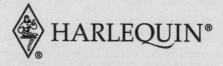

HARLEQUIN®

TORONTO • NEW YORK • LONDON
AMSTERDAM • PARIS • SYDNEY • HAMBURG
STOCKHOLM • ATHENS • TOKYO • MILAN • MADRID
PRAGUE • WARSAW • BUDAPEST • AUCKLAND

If you purchased this book without a cover you should be aware that this book is stolen property. It was reported as "unsold and destroyed" to the publisher, and neither the author nor the publisher has received any payment for this "stripped book."

Recycling programs
for this product may
not exist in your area.

ISBN-13: 978-0-373-52762-5

FORGOTTEN MISTRESS, SECRET LOVE-CHILD

First North American Publication 2010.

Copyright © 2009 by Annie West.

All rights reserved. Except for use in any review, the reproduction or utilization of this work in whole or in part in any form by any electronic, mechanical or other means, now known or hereafter invented, including xerography, photocopying and recording, or in any information storage or retrieval system, is forbidden without the written permission of the publisher, Harlequin Enterprises Limited, 225 Duncan Mill Road, Don Mills, Ontario, Canada M3B 3K9.

This is a work of fiction. Names, characters, places and incidents are either the product of the author's imagination or are used fictitiously, and any resemblance to actual persons, living or dead, business establishments, events or locales is entirely coincidental.

This edition published by arrangement with Harlequin Books S.A.

For questions and comments about the quality of this book please contact us at Customer_eCare@Harlequin.ca.

® and TM are trademarks of the publisher. Trademarks indicated with ® are registered in the United States Patent and Trademark Office, the Canadian Trade Marks Office and in other countries.

www.eHarlequin.com

Printed in U.S.A.

FORGOTTEN MISTRESS,
SECRET LOVE-CHILD

This one's for Judy!
Hope it brings you joy.

Warm hugs and huge thanks to
Anna, Josie, Marilyn, Monique and Serena,
whose expertise made this book possible.

CHAPTER ONE

ALESSANDRO spared barely a glance for the promotional material he tossed into his out tray. His newest PA still hadn't learnt what he should see and what he had no time for. The textile manufacturing arm of the company would be represented at the upcoming trade fair. But one of his managers could handle that. It hardly needed the CEO to…

Oddio mio!

His gaze caught on a photo as a brochure landed askew, half covered by discarded papers.

Alessandro's eyes narrowed on the curve of a woman's smile, a tiny mole like a beauty spot drawing attention to a mouth that would catch any man's interest. Wide, lush, inviting.

Every muscle froze even as his pulse revved and blood roared in his ears.

That smile.

That mouth.

Yet it wasn't sexual awareness that arrested him. A tantalising wisp of almost-memory wafted behind his conscious thoughts. A taste, sweet as ripe summer cherries, rich and addictive.

Heat filled him, despite the climate-controlled air in his spacious office. A zap of something that might have been emotion stifled the breath in his lungs. Alessandro froze, telling himself not to analyse but to relax and let the sensations surface. *Willing* the recollections to come.

Like a lacy curtain in a breeze, the blankness cloaking his memory of those missing months two years ago rippled. It shifted, parted, and then dropped back into place.

His hands clenched, white-knuckled on the edge of his glass and black marble desk. But Alessandro didn't register pain, just the infuriating, familiar sense of nothingness.

Only to himself would he acknowledge how helpless that void made him feel. How vulnerable. It didn't matter that he'd been assured those lost months contained nothing out of the ordinary. Other people remembered that time: what he'd done and said. But he, Alessandro Mattani, had no recall.

Swift as thought, he tugged the brochure from the papers. It was an advertisement for a luxury hotel. He turned it over. A luxury hotel in Melbourne.

Alessandro waited, but no spark of recognition came. He hadn't travelled to Melbourne.

Not that he could remember.

Impatience flared and he forced it down, breathing deeply. An emotional response wouldn't help. Even if the sense of loss, of missing something vital, sometimes threatened to drive him to the edge.

He flipped over the flyer again. A woman, a receptionist, smiled at a handsome couple as they checked in. The photo was professionally styled, yet despite its air-brushed gloss, there was something riveting about the receptionist's smile.

The setting was opulent, but Alessandro had grown up with luxury and barely bothered to notice. The woman, on the other hand…she intrigued him.

The more he stared, the more he felt an atavistic premonition that made his blood pump faster and prickled the skin at his nape. She was so familiar.

Had she smiled at him like that?

A tickle of awareness started low in his belly.

A tickle of…certainty.

Carefully he catalogued her features. Dark hair pulled back sleekly from a pleasant but unremarkable face. Her nose was pert, a trifle short. Her eyes were surprisingly light for her brunette colouring. Her mouth was wide.

She wasn't beautiful. She wasn't exotic enough to turn heads. And yet she had…something. A charisma the photographer had seen and capitalised on.

Alessandro traced the angle of her cheekbone, the gentle curve of her jaw, to pause on the lush promise of her lips.

There it was again. That tingle of presentiment. The intuition that she was no stranger. It drew every muscle and sinew in his body tight, as if in readiness for action.

Behind the opaque gauze of his faulty memory something shifted.

Sensation, soft as the tentative brush of those lips against his. That taste again, of sun-ripened cherries. Irresistible. The phantom caress of delicate fingers along his jaw, over his rapidly pulsing heart. The sound of feminine sighs, the aftermath of ecstasy.

Alessandro's chest heaved as if from intense physical exertion. Sweat prickled his nape and brow as his body stirred with arousal.

Impossible!

Yet instinct clamoured with a truth he couldn't ignore.

He knew her. Had met her. Held her. Made love to her.

His nostrils flared on a surge of wholly masculine possessiveness. The primitive sense of ownership, of a male scenting his mate, was unmistakeable.

He stared at the image of a stranger from the other side of the world. If he hadn't visited Melbourne, had she travelled here to Lombardia?

Frustration at those missing months simmered.

For long minutes Alessandro considered the photograph, his thumb absently caressing the curve of her cheek.

Impossible as it seemed, the certainty grew that this woman held the key to his locked memories. Could she open them? Restore what he'd lost and obliterate the sense that he was somehow less than he'd been. The gnawing hint of dissatisfaction with his world.

Alessandro reached for the phone. He intended to have answers, no matter what it took.

'Thanks, Sarah, you're a lifesaver.' Relief flooded Carys. Today everything that could go wrong had. At least this one thing, the most important, was sorted.

'No worries,' her neighbour and babysitter responded. 'Leo will be fine staying over.'

Carys knew Sarah was right, but that didn't stop the twinge of regret, sharp in her chest. When she'd taken this job at the Landford Hotel it was with the expectation she'd be home most days at a reasonable hour. Early enough to look after her son.

She didn't want Leo growing used to an absentee parent too busy with her career to spend time with him. The sort of home life Carys had taken for granted as a child.

Especially since Leo only had her.

The twinge beneath her breast intensified, catching her breath as pain ripped through her. Even after all this time she couldn't suppress the shaft of regret and longing that pierced her whenever she remembered.

She needed to toughen up. Once upon a time she'd chased her dream, but she wasn't fool enough to believe in it any more. Not after she'd learned so cruelly how futile that dream was.

'Carys? What's wrong?'

'Nothing.' Hastily she forced a smile, knowing Sarah could read her tone even over the phone. 'I owe you one.'

'You sure do. You can babysit for us next weekend. We've got plans for a night on the town, if you can mind Ashleigh.'

'Done.' She looked at her watch. She had to get back before the next crisis hit. 'Don't forget to give Leo a goodnight kiss from me.' Stupid to feel that catch in her throat because tonight she wouldn't feed him his evening meal or kiss his plump pink cheek at bedtime.

Her son was in good hands and, she told herself sternly, she was lucky to have landed a job that usually gave her regular time with him. She was grateful the management had been impressed enough to allow her reasonably family-friendly hours.

Today was the exception. The flu that ravaged the Landford's staff had hit at the worst possible time. More than a third of the staff was off sick just when there was a series of major functions.

It didn't matter that Carys had already spent more than a full day on the job. The collapse just an hour ago of David, the senior functions manager, with a soaring temperature, meant Carys had to step into that role too.

Nerves fluttered in her stomach. This was her chance to prove herself and justify David's faith in her, having taken her on despite her incomplete qualifications. He'd been a good friend and a terrific mentor. She owed him not only her position, but the hard-won self-confidence she'd slowly built since coming to Melbourne.

'I don't know what time I'll be back, Sarah. Probably in the early hours.' Steadfastly Carys refused to worry about how she'd manage the trip home. She couldn't rely on public transport at that time, and the cost of a cab was prohibitive. 'I'll see you around breakfast time, if that's OK?'

'That's fine, Carys. Don't fret. We'll see you when we see you.'

Slowly Carys replaced the phone and stretched her hunched shoulders. She'd been working at the computer and on the phone without a break for so long her body ached all over.

She glanced at the monitor before her and saw the lines of the spreadsheet she'd opened dance and jumble before her eyes. She pinched the bridge of her nose, knowing that no matter how hard she concentrated, working on the document would be a test of endurance and determination.

Sighing, she reached for her tinted reading glasses and leaned forward.

She had to finish this. Only then could she make last minute checks on the arrangements for tonight's masked ball.

Carys stood in the corner of the ballroom near the door to the kitchens, listening to the head waiter's whispered update. It was mayhem in the kitchen with more staff struck down by this virulent flu. Only a couple of the extra waitstaff had arrived to replace those who'd phoned in ill, and the chefs were barely able to cope.

Fortunately, the guests hadn't noticed anything wrong. The

Landford prided itself on superb service, and the staff were doing everything to live up to that reputation.

The ballroom, all black and gold, was gracious and formally elegant. Antique chandeliers sparkled, casting a glow that set jewels scintillating among the A-list crowd. The guests looked impossibly chic as befitted one of Fashion Week's major events.

The room smelled of exclusive fragrances, hothouse flowers and money. Serious money. Celebrities, designers, buyers, the *crème de la crème* of Australian society, were here tonight and plenty of international high-flyers too.

And they were all her responsibility.

Carys' pulse thundered and she struggled to focus on her companion's words. She must concentrate if she wanted to ensure tonight was a success. Too much was at stake.

'All right. I'll see if we can get someone else from the restaurant to help out.' She nodded, dismissing him and turning to the house phone on the wall. She reached out to hit the speed dial number for the restaurant, then froze.

A tingling sensation began at the base of her spine. It burned its way up her back like the slide of hot ice on bare skin. Except her skin wasn't bare. She wore a regulation jacket and straight skirt, dark stockings and high heels.

Yet through the layers of clothing her skin sizzled, the hairs on her neck prickling.

Carys replaced the phone with stiff, unsteady fingers. She pivoted, turning to face the shifting, colourful crowd. Staff circulated with gourmet canapés and vintage champagne; groups broke and reformed.

The guests, most of them wearing exquisite handmade masks, were busy enjoying themselves or networking or showing off their finery. They wouldn't notice anyone who didn't belong in their rarefied circle.

That suited Carys. She didn't hanker for a place at a fairy-tale ball. Not since she'd given up on the whole Prince Charming fantasy.

Yet heat washed her cheeks. Her breath snagged in her throat and her pulse accelerated as instinct told her she was being watched.

Her heart was in her mouth as frantically she searched the throng for something, someone, familiar. Someone who could make her skin tingle and her heart race as it had before, long ago.

Briefly she shut her eyes. Madness! That was in the past. A past best forgotten.

Tiredness and nerves had simply made her imagine things.

Her path and his would never cross again. He'd made certain of that. Carys' lips twisted in a grimace as familiar pain stabbed her chest.

No! Not now. She refused to let her wayward imagination distract her. People depended on her. She had a job to do.

From across the packed room he watched her.

His fingers curled, white-knuckled, around the back of a nearby chair. Blood roared in his ears as his heart thundered out of control. The shock of recognition was so strong he shut his eyes for an instant and lightning flickered across the darkness of his closed lids.

Opening them, he saw her turn to the wall phone, her movements jerky.

It was her. Not just the woman from the brochure, but more, the woman he remembered. Correction—almost remembered.

An image teased his mind. An image of her walking away from him. Her back rigid, her steps staccato bites that ate up the ground as if she couldn't get away fast enough. Bites that echoed the rapid pulse of his drumming heart as he stood rooted to the spot. She carried a case, the taxi driver ahead of her stowing another bag in his vehicle.

Finally she paused. Alessandro's heart stopped and rose in his throat. But she didn't turn around. A moment later she was in the car as it accelerated in a spurt of gravel and swooped away down the private road from his Lake Como home.

Still he stood, prey to an alien mix of sensations. Fury, relief, disappointment, disbelief.

And hurt! Pain filled the yawning chasm inside him.

Only once before in his entire life had Alessandro felt so intensely. At five, when his mother had deserted him for a life of pampered luxury with her lover.

He stirred and shook his head, banishing the misty image, belatedly aware again of the crowded ballroom.

Yet the powerful brew of emotions still stirred in his breast. *Maddona mia!* No wonder he felt vulnerable. Such feelings… Who was this woman to awake such responses in him?

Anger mingled with impatience. That mere chance had led him here. That he could so easily have missed this opportunity to learn more.

Deliberately he flexed his fingers and let go of the chair back, feeling at last the deep imprint of curved wood score his palm.

The wait was over.

He would have his answers now. Tonight.

Surreptitiously Carys slid a foot from her shoe and wriggled her toes. Soon the ball would be over. Then she could oversee the clearing away and setting up for the next day's fashion show.

She suppressed a rising yawn. Every bone in her body ached, and she wanted nothing more than to flop into bed.

She skirted the dance floor. She'd just check on—

A hand, large, warm and insistent took hers, pulling her to a halt. Quickly she summoned a serene expression, ready to deal with the guest who'd overstepped the boundaries by touching her. She hoped he wasn't intoxicated.

Carys had just pinned a small professional smile on her face when a tug of her hand made her turn.

The carefully crafted smile slid away.

For an instant Carys' heart stopped beating as she looked up at the man before her.

Unlike most of the revellers, he still wore his mask. His dark hair was cut brutally short, sculpting a beautifully shaped head. The mask shadowed his eyes, but she caught a gleam of dark fire. His mouth was a grim slash above a strong, firm chin.

Her eyes widened, staring at that chin. It couldn't be…

Then he moved and she caught the faint tang of an unfamiliar cologne. Her heart dived.

Of course it wasn't him!

A scar snaked up his brow from the edge of the mask. The

man she'd known had been as devastatingly handsome as a young god. No scars. His complexion had been golden too, olive, gilded by hours in the sun, not as pale as this stranger's.

And yet…

And yet she stupidly wished in that moment it was him. Against all logic and the need to protect herself, how badly she wanted it to be so.

Carys drew herself up straighter, fumbling for poise while her nerves screamed with disappointment.

He was tall, far taller than she, even though she wore heels. Surely as tall as… No! She wasn't going there. Wasn't playing that pathetic game any more.

'Can I help you?' The words emerged huskily, more like an intimate invitation than a cool query.

Silently she cursed the way he'd thrown her off balance just by reminding her of a time, and a man, best forgotten.

'I think you've mistaken me for someone else.' She rushed into speech again, needing to rein in wayward thoughts. Her words were clipped, though she was careful not to reveal her annoyance. If she could extricate herself without a fuss, she would.

Carys tugged her hand but his grip firmed and he drew her forward. She stumbled, surprised by his implacable hold.

Tilting her head up, she looked him in the eye. She expected him to comment on the food or the music, or demand assistance in some way.

Instead his silence unnerved her.

Her skin grew tight as the illusion grew that they stood alone, cut off from the others.

Around them conversation buzzed, music swirled, and a tinkle of feminine laughter sounded. But the man in the perfectly cut dinner jacket, with the perfectly cut jaw, said nothing. Just held her.

Heat flared under her skin as again instinct shouted a warning to beware.

His hold shifted and his thumb slid over the sensitive place between her thumb and forefinger. A spike of heat transfixed her. Her eyes widened as a tremor echoed through the secret recesses of her body.

'You need to let me go.' She lifted her chin higher, wishing she could see his eyes properly.

He inclined his head, and the breath she hadn't known she held whooshed out. See? He probably just wanted something mundane like another bottle of wine for his table.

She opened her mouth to enquire when someone bumped her, propelling her towards the hard male torso before her.

Carys heard a muffled apology but barely noticed.

Large hands grasped her upper arms. In front of her stretched an expanse of exquisitely tailored elegance, that ultra-masculine chin with just the hint of a cleft and a pair of shoulders to make any woman sit up and take notice.

Shoulders just like…

Carys bit her lip. This had to end.

This was a *stranger.* So he had shoulders to die for and a jaw that seemed achingly familiar. The gold signet ring on his finger was one she'd never seen. And, despite the similar height, he was leaner than the man she'd known.

Another couple buffeted her, talking volubly as they passed. Suddenly she found herself plastered against a hard body that seemed all heat and raw strength. Her senses whirled in a giddy riot.

She imagined she could feel each muscle of his body against hers. Beneath the expensive cologne an elusive undertone of warm male skin tickled her nostrils and she inhaled sharply. He was too familiar, like a phantom from one of the endless dreams that haunted her.

His odd silence intensified her sense of unreality.

Then his hold shifted. A hand slid down her back, poised almost possessively just above her bottom, long fingers spread. Heat roared in the pit of her belly. The heat of desire. A sensation she hadn't felt, it seemed, in a lifetime.

Her body responded to the ultra-masculine allure of his, softening, trembling—

'I need to go.' Carys jerked her head back from the muscled chest that drew her like a magnet. 'Please!'

Her mouth trembled in a wobbly grimace, and to her dismay

hot tears prickled her eyes. Part of her yearned crazily to succumb to his potent maleness.

Because he reminded her of the one man who had taught her the dangers of instant physical attraction.

She had to get out of here.

With a strength born of desperation, she wrenched herself free and stumbled back, off balance when he released her instantly.

Carys took a shaky step away, then another.

The man in the dark mask watched her, eyes unreadable, his body as still as a predator about to pounce.

Her throat squeezed tight in inexplicable panic. She opened her mouth but no sound came. Then she spun and blindly forced her way through the crowd.

Wearily Carys tucked a strand of hair behind her ear. The last of the guests had finally gone and the vast ballroom was empty but for the staff tidying up and moving furniture.

The chirrup of a house phone snagged her attention. She found herself crossing her fingers that there were no more problems. Not tonight, correction, this morning. She was running on empty.

She was still unsettled by the memory of the stranger. The man who'd seemed so familiar yet couldn't be.

'Hello?'

'Carys? Glad I caught you.' She recognised the new guy on night duty at reception. 'You've got an urgent call. I'll connect you.'

Instantly all weariness vanished at the sound of those dreaded words 'urgent call'. Carys' stomach dropped and fear filled the void. Was it Leo? An illness? An accident?

She twisted a button on her jacket, waiting breathlessly for bad news as her nerves stretched taut.

It would be tonight of all nights that something went wrong. She should have found a way to get home earlier.

The click of the new connection was loud in her ears. As was the silence that followed, a waiting silence.

'Sarah? What's wrong? What's happened?'

There was a pause in which she heard the echo of her own breathing.

Then a voice like black velvet emerged.

'Carys.'

Just one word and every hair on her body rose. It was the voice that haunted her dreams. A voice that, despite everything, still had the power to thicken her blood, turning it to warm treacle.

Her knees buckled and she found herself sitting on the edge of a table that had been moved up against the wall.

Her fingers splayed over her throat in a desperate gesture of vulnerability.

It couldn't be!

Her mouth opened and her throat worked, but no sound emerged.

'We need to meet,' said the voice of her past. 'Now.'

CHAPTER TWO

'WHO is this?' Carys' voice emerged as a raw croak.

It couldn't be.

Not here. Not now.

Not after she'd finally convinced herself she never wanted to see him again. Fate couldn't be so cruel.

Yet some wayward self-destructive impulse sent a buzz of excitement skimming along her nerves. Once she'd longed for him to make contact, to come after her, tell her he'd been wrong. Tell her…no, she wasn't so credulous as to believe in such fantasies any more.

What did he want? Her hand tightened like a claw at her throat. A premonition of danger filled her, icing her blood.

'You know who it is, Carys.' Just the way he pronounced her name with that sexy Italian accent turned the word into a caress that melted her insides.

He'd always threatened her self-control. Carys remembered murmured enticements in that dark coffee voice and how he'd persuaded her to give up everything she'd worked for just for the privilege of being with him.

Fool!

She shivered and sat up straighter, berating herself.

'Please identify yourself,' she said tersely.

It couldn't be him. He'd never follow her to Australia. He'd made that clear when she'd left with her tail between her legs.

But the memory of the stranger tonight at the ball, the masked

man who'd made her think of *him*, battered at her disbelief.
Wildly she shook her head, trying to clear a brain overloaded by
exhaustion and stress.

Was she going mad? Seeing him, even hearing him, when she
knew perfectly well he was ensconced in his oh-so-exclusive
world of rich, elegant, aristocratic friends. Of high-flying
business deals and blue blood and glamour.

Where people like her only provided brief amusement.

'Don't pretend not to know me, Carys. I have no time for
puerile games.' He paused as if waiting for her to rush into
speech. 'It's Alessandro Mattani.'

Silence throbbed as she clutched the receiver. Her heart
crashed against her ribs. She would have slid to the floor if she
hadn't already been sitting.

'Alessandro…'

'Mattani. I'm sure you recognise the name.' His voice was
sharp as a razor.

Recognise the name! Once she'd even hoped to share it with him.

A bubble of hysterical laughter threatened to explode from her
stiff lips. Carys slapped her palm across her mouth, concentrat-
ing on deep breaths. She needed oxygen.

The room spun crazily and dark spots whirled in her vision.

A clatter jerked her back to full awareness, and she looked
down as if from an enormous distance to see the phone had
slipped from her nerveless fingers onto the table.

Alessandro Mattani.

The man she'd loved.

The man who'd broken her heart.

A sound caught her attention and Carys looked up, suddenly
aware again of her surroundings. The last of the staff were
leaving and waving goodnight.

Belatedly she lifted a hand in acknowledgement.

Dazedly she looked around. The stage was set for tomorrow's fashion show. Enormous jardinières with arrangements of exotic orchids and jungle greenery had been
strategically positioned as she'd instructed. The lights were
dimmed and she was alone.

But for the voice on the other end of the line. The voice of her dreams.

Tentatively, as if reaching out to touch an untamed animal, Carys stretched her fingers to the phone. She lifted it, and a deep voice barked in her ear.

'Carys?'

'I'm here.'

Silence, but for the impatient hiss of indrawn breath.

'No more games. I want to see you.'

Well, bully for him. She was past the stage of worrying what Alessandro Mattani wanted.

Besides, she wasn't foolish enough to go near him again. Even now she didn't trust her hard-won defences against the man who'd only had to smile and crook his finger to get what he wanted from her. She'd surrendered her job, all her plans, even her self-respect to be with him.

Carys stiffened her spine and braced her palm on the table beside her.

'That's not possible.'

'Of course it's possible,' he bit out. 'I'm just twelve floors away.'

Twelve floors? Her heart galloped faster. Here, in Melbourne? At the Landford?

Her gaze swerved to the edge of the dance floor, instinct and disbelief warring.

'That *was* you tonight? At the ball?' If she'd been less stunned, she might have cared about how much her strained voice revealed. But she was battling shock. She had no thought to spare for pride.

He didn't answer.

Heat sparked low in her abdomen and washed through her like a flood tide. It *had* been him. He'd held her in his arms.

How often had she yearned for his embrace? Despite what she'd told herself about forgetting the past.

He'd held her and she hadn't known him?

But she had, hadn't she? Despite the new cologne, the paleness of his once-golden skin, the scar.

Fear jolted through her, stealing her breath.

He'd been hurt! How badly? Urgent questions clamoured on her tongue.

Shakily Carys gathered the tattered remnants of control. She ignored the unspoken questions, opting for the most important one.

'What do you want?' Her voice sounded stretched too thin, like beaten metal about to snap under pressure.

'I've already told you.' Impatience threaded his words. 'To see you.'

She couldn't prevent a snort of disbelief at his words. How times had changed.

Finally pride came to her rescue.

'It's late. I've had a long day and I'm going home. There's nothing more to say between us.' Tentatively she slipped her feet to the floor, waiting to see if her legs would collapse under her.

'Are you sure?' His words, soft and deep like the alpine eiderdowns they'd once shared, brushed across her senses. His voice was alive with erotic undercurrents.

She jerked upright.

Flame licked that secret needy place deep inside her, the place that had been cold and empty ever since she'd left him. The realisation drew her anger.

No, she wasn't sure. That was the hell of it.

'I'm in the presidential suite,' he said after a moment. 'I'll expect you in ten minutes.'

'You have no right to give me orders.' Belatedly she found her voice.

'You don't wish to meet me?' Incredulity coloured his tone.

Had he never had a knock-back from a woman?

Certainly not from her. She'd been putty in his elegant, powerful hands from the instant she'd fallen head over heels for him.

'The past is the past.' At the last moment she prevented herself saying his name. She didn't want the sound of it on her lips. It was too intimate, evoked too many memories.

'Perhaps so. But *I* wish to meet *you.*' His tone made it clear that he wasn't about to go down on bended knee and beg her forgiveness.

Carys rubbed her forehead. The very thought of Alessandro, darling of the jet set, commercial power-broker and hundred percent red-hot macho Italian male on his knees before any woman was ludicrous.

'You have ten minutes,' he reiterated.

'And if I don't come?'

He took his time responding. 'That's your choice, Ms Wells.' His formality in that silky smooth voice held more threat than any bluster. Or was that her imagination?

'I have personal matters to discuss. I thought you'd prefer to do that in the privacy of my suite. Of course, I can see you instead during business hours tomorrow.' He paused. 'I understand you share an office with colleagues? Presumably they won't be inconvenienced by our conversation.'

He left the sentence dangling and Carys bit her lip, imagining how her workmates would react to Alessandro and his *personal matters.*

'No doubt your manager won't mind you taking time off to deal with a private matter,' he purred in that outrageously delicious accent. 'Even though I understand you're only here on an extended probation?'

Carys' jaw dropped. He'd had her records investigated! How else could he know about her long probation period since she'd been employed without completing her qualifications?

Those employment details were supposed to be confidential.

Her defensive hackles rose as the old sense of inadequacy surfaced. Of not being good enough. Not making the grade. And more, of being cornered, facing an implacable, unstoppable force that threatened to overpower her.

Defeat tasted bitter on her tongue.

Or was that fear? Fear that, despite his initial rejection, Alessandro had come to take Leo from her.

Her shoulders tightened.

'Ten minutes,' she confirmed.

Alessandro stood at the full-length window, staring across the Yarra River to the lights of Melbourne's cityscape.

He didn't see them. Instead his brain conjured an image of blue-grey eyes, wide and apparently guileless.

He shifted as heat shot through his body straight from his groin at the memory of her soft body nestled against him.

From the moment he'd sighted her across the ballroom, he'd known. The awareness he'd experienced looking at her photo was nothing compared with tonight's instant gut-deep certainty.

This woman was his.

Alessandro tossed back the espresso his butler had brewed, feeling the shot of caffeine in his blood.

His earlier flash of memory told him they hadn't parted amicably. Hell, she'd walked out on him! No other lover had ever done that.

Yet he knew with absolute certainty there was still something between them. Something that accounted for the nagging dissatisfaction that had plagued him since the accident.

Why had they separated?

He intended to discover everything about the yawning blankness that was his memory of the months preceding his accident.

He refused to let her escape till he had answers.

From the moment he'd held her, the sense of unfinished business between them had been overwhelming. Even now he felt the low-grade hum of awareness, waiting for her.

There was more too. Not just the immediate sense of connection and possessiveness. There was an inner turmoil that surely must be long-dormant emotions.

He'd watched her, listened to her, and been dumbstruck by the intensity of his conflicting feelings.

Alessandro had harnessed all his willpower to drive himself to recover from his injuries and turn around the faltering family business. He'd blocked out everything but the need to haul the company from the brink of disaster. Everything else had been a pallid blur.

Until now no one had come close to breaking through his guarded self-possession. Not his step-mother, not the many women angling for his attention. Not his friends.

Despite his wide social circle, he was a loner like his father.

The old man had isolated himself, focusing only on business after his first wife's betrayal and desertion.

As a result Alessandro had learned the Mattani way early, concealing his boyish grief and bewilderment behind a façade. Over the years that façade of calm had become reality. He'd developed the knack of repressing strong emotions, distancing himself from personal vulnerability.

Until tonight. When he'd come face to face with Carys Wells. And he'd...*felt* things. A stirring of discontent, desire, loss.

He frowned. He had no time for emotions.

Lust, yes. He was no stranger to physical desire. That was easily assuaged. But the disturbing sensations churning in his belly were unfamiliar, caused by something more complex.

A knock sounded on the door. Grateful for the interruption to his unpalatable thoughts, Alessandro put down his cup and turned as the butler crossed the foyer.

Alessandro was surprised to register his shoulders stiffening, locking as tension hardened his stance.

Since when had he, Alessandro Mattani, experienced nerves? Even when the specialists had shaken their heads over his injuries, referring to complications and a long convalescence, all he'd felt was impatience to get out of hospital. Especially when he'd learned the impact his accident, so soon after his father's death, had caused.

The commercial vultures had begun circling, ready to take advantage of the mistakes his father had made in those last months and of Alessandro's incapacity.

'Ms Wells, sir.' The butler ushered her into the sitting room.

She stood as if poised for flight, just inside the door. Once more that shock of connection smacked him square in the chest. He rocked back on his feet.

Jerkily she lifted a hand to smooth her hair, then dropped it as she caught his scrutiny.

Tension, palpable and vibrating, strung out between their locked gazes.

Carys Wells looked out of place in the opulence of Melbourne's most exclusive hotel suite. Unless, of course, she was here to provide a personal service to the occupant. Delivering a message or bringing room service.

Alessandro's thoughts jagged on the sort of *personal* service he'd like her to provide.

It didn't matter that he knew any number of more beautiful women. Clever, high achievers who combined chic style, business savvy and an eagerness to share his bed.

Something about Carys set her apart.

Her curves would horrify the perpetually dieting women he knew in Milano. Her dark hair was severely styled, if you could call scraping it back into a bun a style. Her make-up was discreet, and she wore a sensible navy suit that no woman of his acquaintance would be seen dead in.

Yet the way her face had lit with emotion earlier hinted at a more subtle attractiveness. And those legs... The sight of her shapely calves and trim ankles in high heels and dark stockings tugged at his long-dormant libido.

Alessandro's hands flexed. He wanted to explore further, to discover if her legs were as sexy all the way up.

Instinct—or was it memory?—told him her legs were superb. Just as he knew he'd found pleasure in her neatly curved figure and her deliciously full lips.

Belatedly he dragged his gaze from the woman who'd lured him halfway around the world.

The way she sidetracked him was unprecedented. One way or another he had to get her out of his system.

'*Grazie,* Robson. That's all for tonight.'

The butler inclined his head. 'There are refreshments on the sideboard should you require them, sir, madam.' Not by so much as a flicker did he indicate he knew the woman before him to be a co-worker. Then he moved silently away towards the kitchen and the staff entrance.

'Please—' Alessandro gestured to the nearby lounge '—take a seat.'

For a moment he thought she wasn't going to accept. Finally she walked across the antique carpet to sit in a cavernous wing chair. The glow of lamps lit her face, revealing a tension around her pursed lips he hadn't noticed before. She looked tired.

Alessandro flicked a look at his watch. It was very late. He'd become accustomed to working long into the night, fuelled by caffeine and his own formidable drive.

Conscience niggled. He should have left this till tomorrow. But he'd been unable to ignore the edgy frustration that drove him relentlessly. He was so close he couldn't rest till he had answers from her.

He'd already been stymied once. Alessandro had confronted her at the ball only to find he'd been robbed of composure and even the power of speech by a shocking blast of recognition. He'd frozen, the one thought in his atrophying mind to hold her and not let her go.

The completeness of that instant of vulnerability had stunned and shamed him. *Never* had he felt at such a loss. Not in business. Definitely not in his dealings with women.

Now he was himself once more. It would not happen again. *Alessandro Mattani did not do vulnerable.*

He thrust aside the momentary doubt at his tactics and strode across to the sideboard.

'Tea, coffee?' he offered. 'Wine?'

'I don't want anything.' She sat straighter, her chin hitched high in unspoken defiance. That spark of rebellion brought colour to her cheeks and made her eyes sparkle.

Alessandro paused, watching fascinated as she transformed from drab to intriguing in an instant. Then he turned, poured himself a small measure of cognac, and took a seat opposite her.

All the while she watched him with those luminous eyes that had captivated him the moment he saw her.

What did she see? Was she cataloguing the differences in him? It surprised him to discover how much he wanted to read her thoughts. Know what she felt. Did she too experience this gnawing tension, like an ache between the ribs?

'I see you've noticed my scar.'

The wash of colour along her cheekbones intensified, but she didn't look away. Nor did she respond.

Alessandro wasn't vain enough to worry about his marred face. Besides, it was his wealth and position as much as his looks to which women responded. They might say they wanted a man of charm or kindness, but he knew how fickle they were. Neither marriage vows nor ties of blood between mother and child could hold them when they found someone who offered more wealth and prestige.

That didn't bother Alessandro. He had both in abundance. If ever he wanted a woman permanently he'd have his pick. Some time in the future. Not now.

He swirled the fine brandy in its glass, inhaling its mellow scent.

'Am I so repulsive, then?' He shot her a look that dared her to prevaricate.

Repulsive? Carys wished he were. Then maybe she could tear her gaze away. Her heart hammered. She struggled to hide her shortened breathing as she felt the tug of his potent masculine aura.

It had always been the same. But she'd prayed time and common sense would cure her of the fatal weakness.

She met his intense moss-green gaze, recognised the way his thick dark lashes shadowed his eyes. His eyelids dropped as if to hide his thoughts. The familiarity of that expression, as much as its banked heat, made her insides squirm in mixed delight and distress.

'You got me here to talk about your looks?' Carys had more sense than to answer his question.

To her horror she found him more attractive than ever. Even the scar leading from just beneath one straight black eyebrow up to his temple failed to detract from the beautiful spare lines of his leanly sculpted face.

She gripped her hands tight in her lap, alarmed to discover that, when it came to pure animal attraction, Alessandro still exerted a power she couldn't deny.

Just as well she had more sense than to succumb to it. She was cured. Surely she was.

'You keep staring at it.' He lifted the brandy to his lips. Carys watched the movement of his throat as he swallowed and her pulse tripped crazily. She'd rarely seen him in formal clothes, but they only enhanced his magnetism.

Alessandro had been an enigma, suave and sophisticated, impossibly elegant even in the most casual clothes, even *without* clothes. But at the same time there'd been something earthy and all-male about him. Something innately stronger than the varnish of wealth and centuries of good breeding.

'What are you thinking?' he asked.

Heat flared in her cheeks as Carys realised she was imagining him naked, long-limbed and strong. She tore her gaze away.

She might despise him, but she was still woman enough to respond to his sheer sex appeal.

'Nothing. I was just thinking about how you've changed.' It was only half a lie.

'Have I altered so much?' She sensed movement and turned her head to find him leaning forward, elbows on his knees.

She shrugged. 'It's been…' Just in time she stopped herself. He didn't need to know she recalled to the day how long it had been. 'A while. People change.'

'How have I changed?'

Carys wondered at the intensity of his stare. She felt it like the caress of a jade blade across her skin, smooth but potentially lethal.

'Well, there's the scar for a start.'

She closed her lips before she could blurt out questions about his health. Had he been in an accident? Or, her thudding heartbeat faltered, had it been surgery?

Sternly she told herself she didn't care.

'I'm in excellent health now.' The murmured words surprised her. How had he read her mind?

'Of course you are,' she said too quickly. 'Otherwise you wouldn't be here.' If he was ill he'd be in Italy, under the care of the country's top doctors, not summoning her to his room in the early hours to talk about…what *did* he want?

Carys' nerves spasmed in denial. There could only be one reason for his presence. Only one thing he wanted.

Her son.

Surely Alessandro's presence here meant he'd decided belatedly that he wanted Leo after all.

Alessandro didn't do things by halves. If he wanted something he'd take it all. And surely any normal Italian male would want his own son?

Fear wrapped icy fingers around her heart. If she was right, what chance did she have of stopping him?

'How else have I changed?'

Carys frowned at this fixation with his looks. The man she'd known had been careless about that, though he'd dressed with the instinctive panache of one who'd grown up amongst a chic, fashion-conscious set.

'You're paler than before. And thinner.'

When they'd met, he'd been on a skiing holiday, his olive skin burnished dark golden-brown by the alpine sun. His body was all hard-packed muscle and rangy height. Carys had looked into his dancing green eyes and sensuous smile that made her feel she was the only other person on the planet. Without a second thought she'd fallen for him like a ton of bricks.

Now he seemed pared down, but that only emphasised his spectacular bone structure. The way he moved made it clear he hadn't lost his whipcord strength and abundant energy.

He lifted the brandy to his lips again, but not before she read a wry grimace. 'I've been working long hours.'

Such long hours he'd stopped eating?

Carys looked away, silently berating herself for caring.

'Some things don't change, then.'

Those last weeks, Alessandro had used work as an excuse not to be with her. At first she'd thought there was a problem with the business, or with Alessandro assuming its control after his father's death, but her tentative questions, her attempts to understand and offer support, had been firmly rebuffed.

The company was fine. He was fine. She worried too much. He just had responsibilities to fulfil. She remembered the litany.

Methodically Alessandro had shut her out of his life, day by day and hour by hour. Till their only communication was during the brief pre-dawn hours when he'd take her with a blistering-hot passion that had threatened to consume them both.

Until she'd discovered it wasn't just business taking him away. That he'd had time for other things, other…people. How gullible she'd been, believing he'd be content with the naïve, unsophisticated woman who shared his bed…

'Being the CEO of a multi-national enterprise requires commitment.'

'I know that.' She'd given up worrying about the ridiculous hours he'd begun working. Given up trying to understand what had happened to the charming, attentive man with whom she'd fallen in love. That man had worked hard too, but he'd known how to switch off. How to enjoy being with her.

Her stomach churned. Whatever they'd once shared was over. He'd left her in no doubt she'd never live up to his exacting standards.

What was she doing here?

Her throat closed as the futility of their conversation swamped her. This could lead nowhere, achieve nothing but the reopening of painful wounds.

Carys shot to her feet. 'It's been…interesting seeing you again. But I have to go. It's late.'

The words were barely out of her mouth when he was before her, looming so close she had to tilt her head to meet his eyes. His gaze licked like flame across her skin.

Instinctively she stepped back, only to find her way blocked. Heat engulfed her as her brain processed frantic messages. Of surprise. Of anger. Of excitement.

'You can't leave yet.'

'I can and will.' She refused to play the fool for him again. 'We're finished.'

'Finished?' One straight brow quirked up, and his mouth curved in a tight, unamused smile. 'Then what about this?'

He snagged her close with one long arm so she landed hard against him. Then he lowered his head.

CHAPTER THREE

'ALESSANDRO!'

Her voice was scratchy with surprise as she said his name for the first time, making him pause. Yet the sound was familiar. He felt it deep in his bones.

She was familiar, the way her body melded to his, all feminine enticement as he pinioned her to him.

He'd tried to hold back. Go slow. Behave sensibly.

But from the moment she'd walked in everything had changed. His caution, his adherence to the niceties of social behaviour had melted away. Now he operated on raw, primal instinct that overrode logic and convention.

He held her satisfyingly close. With her breasts cushioned against his torso, her hips pressed against him. He felt anticipation surge.

When she'd arrived, looking weary yet defiant, he'd questioned his need to confront her tonight. But those doubts disintegrated as her body softened against his and he heard the tell-tale hitch in her breathing.

There might be fire in her eyes, but the way she fitted against him belied her indignation.

This was mutual.

He had no conscious recollection of her but his body remembered her. The stirring in his loins told its own tale of familiarity and desire.

He looked down into grey-blue eyes, darkening with sparks

of azure and indigo, and felt he was falling through mist, towards a bright sunny place.

He inhaled her spicy soft cinnamon fragrance and his brain cried *Yes! This is the one!*

'Alessandro!' Her voice was more determined now, like her hands pushing at his chest. Yet that underpinning note of hesitancy betrayed her.

He lifted one hand to palm her face. Her cheek was soft and pale as milk. Her eyelids fluttered and drooped then snapped wide open.

'You have no right to do this. Let me go.' Yet she'd stopped struggling, merely stood straighter and unyielding in his embrace.

'No right?' He swiped his thumb across her mouth, tugging at her lower lip, feeling its luscious pad and the moist heat of her breath against his skin.

Her mouth opened and those eyelids flickered betrayingly.

Tendrils of fire twisted and coiled through his body, unfurling and spreading as he watched her response to that simple caress.

He widened his stance, surrounding her with his thighs and pulling her closer to his pelvis.

The promise of bliss was a primitive tattoo in his blood, pounding heavier, faster, demanding action. Yet Alessandro reined in the impulse to demand more. He had to know, to understand, as well as feel.

'You give me the right when you respond to me that way.' Again he slid his thumb along her mouth, this time pressing deeper till he felt her tongue slick against his finger.

He stiffened, every muscle clamped tight at the roiling surge of need that engulfed him.

Madonna mia! How potent was this woman, that the mere touch of her tongue could splinter his control?

Surprise darkened her eyes. She felt it too.

'I'm not…doing anything,' she protested in a hoarse voice that told its own story. Suddenly she was pushing at him again, trying to lever herself away.

'Carys.' He loved the sound of her name on his tongue. Just as he anticipated, he was addicted to the taste of her lips. 'Would you deny me? Deny this?'

Deftly he slid his hand round to cup her head, feeling the silky weight of her hair against his palm. Then he drew her close, bending to meet her lips.

She turned her head, refusing access to her mouth. His senses filled with the velvet softness of her skin, the sweet temptation of her body's perfume, as he brushed his lips below her ear.

Her restless movements stopped instantly. Arrested by the same sensations that bombarded him? Desire and heady bliss?

He slid his mouth over her neck, then up to her ear, circling the delicate lobe with his tongue.

She started in his arms as if zapped by the same jolt of energy that skewered him to the spot. Through the pounding in his ears he half heard, half felt her sigh.

'You can't deny this,' he murmured.

Her skin tasted clean and sweet, like spring flowers made of flesh. Hungrily he nuzzled the corner of her jaw, the edge of her chin, the beauty spot beside her mouth.

Bracing to pull back just a fraction, he looked down into her face.

His lips curved in a tight, satisfied smile when he saw closed eyes, lips parted invitingly, as if urging him to claim her.

Her hair had started to come down as she tried to avoid his grip. Now, looking at the long strands of wavy silk falling across his wrist, he realised it wasn't black as he'd thought in the ballroom. It was darkest brown, tinged with sparks of russet fire.

An image filled his brain, of rich dark hair spread over plump white pillows. Of his hands threading through its satiny splendour, splaying it out like a radiant sunburst.

Not just an image.

A memory!

Of Carys, lying sleepily in bed with him. Of her lazy smile, so dazzling it rivalled the brilliance of the snow-lit scene visible through the window above the bed.

The impact of that sudden recollection rocked him off balance, his arms tightening automatically around her.

For the second time in one night he'd remembered!

He'd known coming here was right.

With this woman he could unlock the closed door to the past.

Restore all that was lost. Once he remembered he'd be free of this lurking awareness of something missing, of something incomplete in his life.

Then he could move on, content with his life again.

'Alessandro.' Her eyes were open now and aware. He read shock there and chagrin in the way she gnawed at her lip. 'Let me go. Please.'

He'd been taught to respect a woman's wishes. The Mattani code of honour was deeply ingrained, and he would never force himself on a woman. But it was too late to dissemble. Carys wanted this as much as he, despite her words.

Surely one kiss couldn't hurt.

'After this,' he murmured. 'I promise you'll enjoy it.' Almost as much as he intended to.

He captured her head, turned her face up to his, and slanted his mouth over hers.

Carys strained to shove him away. Desperation lent power to her tired limbs, yet she made no impact on him. If anything his wide shoulders loomed closer. He was stronger than her by far.

The knowledge should have frightened her. Yet part of her exulted. The unreformed hedonist inside her that she'd only discovered when she'd met Alessandro. The lover who'd been enraptured by his masculinity and athletic power. The heartbroken woman who'd loved and lost and secretly hoped to have her love returned.

Her struggle was as much within herself as against him.

Warm lips covered her mouth, and a judder of shocking need raked her from head to toe. It was instant, all-consuming and undeniable.

But she refused to give in to it. She pressed her palms against his shoulders and leant back as far as his encompassing arm allowed. Frantic to escape, she remembered too well how she'd always responded to him.

His kiss was unexpectedly tender, a gentle caress of firm lips along the closed line of her mouth.

His unfamiliar cologne, subtle yet masculine, tinged the air.

The heat of his body warmed hers. His arms held her as if he'd never let her go.

Another illusion.

Carys tried to whip up her resolve, her scorn. But her mind fought a losing battle when her body was already capitulating.

'No!' She had to get away. Had to stand firm against him. 'I don't—'

It was too late. With the unerring instinct of a born predator, Alessandro took advantage of her momentary lapse and plunged his tongue into her open mouth.

Her breath stopped as reality splintered into fragments around her. He caressed her tongue, the inside of her cheeks. The dark world behind her closed eyelids came alive with flashes of fire. He grasped the back of her head, then tilted his own so he could delve deeper with a slow thoroughness that made her shudder in response.

Her hands on his shoulders curved, holding tight. Her panic faded. Tentatively her mouth moved with his, following the dance of desire they'd created together time and again. Carys mimicked his movements and slowly, like a sleeper waking from hibernation, felt the life force surge in her blood. Hunger gnawed her belly.

Soon she answered his demands with her own.

This felt so *right*.

His arms curved close, tugging her intimately against him. His kiss lured, delighted and provoked her into a response that escalated from tentative to eager and unashamed.

Now Carys' hands slipped from his shoulders to his neck, then up to furrow through his short, crisp hair and mould his head with desperate fingers. He was real, solid and wonderful, not the ephemeral phantom of her dreams. She needed him close, closer, to satisfy the burgeoning craving for more.

Heady, half-formed memories bombarded her. Of Alessandro pleasuring her. Of him holding her tight in his arms as if he'd never let her go. Of the instant spark of recognition and understanding that had passed between them the moment they'd met.

But these were tiny flickers, mere shadows of thought. She was absorbed in relearning the feel of Alessandro. His hair, his lips and tongue, the hot steel of his arms around her, the muscle and bone strength of his long body. His taste and scent.

Carys leaned in, glorying in the slide of achingly full breasts against his hard torso. She rose on tiptoe, seeking more, trying to get closer, to absorb herself into the wonderful luxury, the effervescent excitement of his kiss.

With a muffled groan, Alessandro lashed his other arm around her, lower, wrapping round her buttocks and lifting her off the ground.

Yes! Carys gave herself up to each exquisite sensation: of their mouths meshing, of his formidable strength enveloping her, of burning hot skin beneath her fingers as she moulded his jaw and cheeks.

Alessandro moved. She felt his thighs shift around her as he walked, and then there was something solid behind her while Alessandro pressed close. A wall? A couch? She'd lost all sense of perspective.

He tilted his hips in a slow grinding movement and desire blasted through her. His pelvis and hers were in perfect alignment, the heavy bulge in his trousers a portent of pleasure to come.

Instinctively she curved her body up to meet him. A throb began deep between her legs, an edgy neediness that strung her tight with anticipation.

'Temptress. Siren.' His muttered words were hoarse, as if squeezed out under duress.

Carys let her head loll against a hard surface and gulped oxygen into her air-starved lungs. Alessandro ravished her face and throat with burning kisses that ignited tiny explosions of pleasure through her taut body. And all the while he pushed close as if he could melt the barrier of their clothes and bring them both the bliss they craved.

One large hand slid down her hip and over her thigh, igniting tremors of fresh awareness. When his palm climbed back, her skirt bunched beneath it, riding higher and higher.

Carys opened her mouth, vaguely aware of the need to protest, but his mouth slammed into hers again, robbing her of breath and the beginnings of thought.

Once more Alessandro pleasured her, this time with a kiss so sweet yet so demanding it devoured the last of her resistance. She lolled back as he drew forth every last shred of hidden longing.

Willingly Carys complied as he lifted her leg up around his hip, and then the other. The bittersweet ache between her legs, and deeper, inside her womb, became a steady throb. Encircling him with her legs, she squeezed tight.

As if he understood, Alessandro pressed close again, pushing his erection just…there.

Yes! That was what she wanted. To have him warm the empty places in her body and her soul that had been chilled for so long.

Large hands slid under the tight, rumpled fabric of her skirt, up her thighs till they reached bare, quivering flesh.

'Stockings,' he breathed against her mouth. 'You dress to drive a man insane.'

She wasn't listening. Carys heard the low burr of his voice, felt his breath against her lips, but the words made no sense. Only the approval in his tone was real.

Haphazardly she ripped at his bow tie, desperate for his hot skin bare beneath her palms.

Long fingers slid around her thighs, stroking and teasing her sensitive skin. She jerked and squirmed, tugging at his shirt till, with a rip, it tore open.

A torrent of slurred Italian signalled his approval. But she barely noticed for heaven was in the touch of wiry hair and steamy satiny flesh under her hands. In the rapid pulse of his heart pounding against her touch.

His hands moved, and a knuckle brushed against the damp cotton of her panties.

'*Cara,*' he growled deep in his throat. 'I *knew* you wanted this as much as I do.' He insinuated probing fingers beneath the elastic of her underwear while, with his other hand, he fumbled at his belt.

Reality, hard and relentless, broke upon her in an instant of icy clarity. The heady, exquisite arousal faded as her mind kicked into gear.

Was it the greedy touch of his fingers in that most intimate of places? The practised way he undid his belt and ripped open the fastening of his trousers? The smug satisfaction in his voice?

He didn't even want *her,* an outraged voice cried in her head. He wanted 'this'. Sex. Physical satisfaction.

Presumably any woman would do. Carys was just conveniently available.

More than available. Willing. Desperate for him.

Aghast, Carys stiffened.

What had she done? She'd let her loneliness, memories of the bliss they'd once shared, lead her into self-destructive temptation.

'No! Stop.' Mortified, she shoved with all her might, wriggling to dislodge his questing fingers and unwrap her legs. 'Let me go!'

She moved so unexpectedly he didn't prevent her and even moved back a precious few centimetres, allowing her to slide her legs free. That was when she registered it was a wall behind her, as her stockinged feet hit the floor. She had to brace herself against the weakness in her knees so she didn't collapse.

He'd almost had her, up against the wall of his suite! Fully clothed!

The glorious heat they'd shared bled away as mortification and disbelief welled. After all that had happened how *could* she have been so weak?

'Carys…'

She batted his hands away, stumbling to escape and tripping over a discarded shoe.

Her self respect was in shreds. Her chest heaved with distress as she fumbled with shaky fingers to push her straight skirt down her hips. Her eyes blurred.

'Let me.'

'No!' Carys whirled to face him, arms outstretched to keep him at bay.

Even with lipstick on his jaw, and his jacket and dress shirt torn open to reveal a dusky, hair-dusted chest, he looked in command, powerful and controlled.

Sexier than any man had a right to be.

Then she saw the way his chest rose and fell, as if from exertion. The tendons in his neck stood out and his facial muscles were drawn too tight. A flush of colour slanted across his cheeks and his nostrils flared as if he fought for oxygen.

The evidence of simple animal lust. That was all Alessandro had ever felt for her.

When would she learn? Self-disgust filled her.

Her poor tortured heart compressed as a weight as big as Flinders Street Station pushed down on her chest. Breathing was agony.

But the realisation of what she'd almost done was worse. One kiss…one kiss and she'd been scrabbling at his shirt, desperate to feel his body against hers, urging him on to take her.

Her chin crumpled and she bit her lip. She'd invited her own degradation.

Once again Alessandro had proved himself a consummate seducer. But that was no excuse. She should be able to resist him. She had to. Where was her self-respect?

'Don't touch me,' she whispered as she wriggled her hips, tugging the skirt down. She kept her eyes above his waist, not wanting to see what she'd felt pressing intimately against her, inviting her to mindless pleasure.

Involuntarily her internal muscles clenched. Her betraying body was still ready for his possession. The knowledge flattened the last remnant of her pride.

'*Va bene.* As you wish.' The feral gleam in Alessandro's eyes warned her he wouldn't be thwarted for long. 'Instead we will talk. For now.'

Fire scorched her throat and she looked away, unable to meet his dark scrutiny any longer.

Slowly Carys backed across the floor, feet sinking into the plush depth of carpet. He didn't follow her but stood, arms akimbo, as if waiting for her to come to her senses.

'We have to talk, Carys.'

Like hell they did. They'd done enough *talking* for one night. The brush of cool air on her heated skin made her frown and reach for her throat, only to discover her blouse hung open to reveal her white cotton bra.

How had that happened? Carys clutched the edges of her

blouse together with numb fingers. She shot an accusing glare across the room, but Alessandro said nothing, merely raised an eyebrow and crossed his arms over his chest as if waiting for her to come to her senses.

For all his immobility she couldn't rid herself of the notion he merely waited to pounce.

Would she have the resolve to stop him next time?

'I'm not staying here to be attacked again.'

'Attacked!' He drew himself up to his full height and stared down his long aristocratic nose at her. 'Hardly that. You were panting for my touch.'

His arrogant claim was the final straw because it was true. Her resolution had failed. She was weak and nothing could protect her from him. Nothing but bluff.

She shrugged, the movement more stiff than insouciant.

'I was curious, that's all. And,' she hurried on as he opened his mouth to reject her explanation, 'and besides, it's been a while since I…'

'You've been saving yourself, *cara?* Is that it?' His smoky voice urged her to assent and blurt out that there'd been no one since him. Wouldn't he just love that!

Fury sizzled along her veins. Glorious wrath at the man who'd taken her innocence, her love and her trust and thought he could have her again at the click of his fingers.

'No,' Carys lied. It would just feed his ego to know there'd been no one since him. She shifted her gaze.

He held her in thrall. What would it take to make him relinquish his pursuit? Desperation drove her to blurt out the first thing she could think of to stop him.

'My boyfriend and I had a disagreement and—'

'Boyfriend?' His voice thundered through the suite. 'You were missing your *boyfriend?* You can't tell me you were thinking of him just now?'

'Can't I?' Carys swung her head round and felt his dark green stare like frozen shards of crystal grazing her skin.

'I don't believe you.' But she'd sown the seed of doubt. That was obvious from his sudden pallor.

A tiny fillip of triumph rose. Maybe she could make herself safe from him after all.

'Believe what you like, Conte Mattani.'

'Don't use that title with me,' he snapped. 'I'm not some stranger.'

She said nothing, merely backed a few more steps towards the foyer.

'You don't intend to leave looking like that,' he announced in a cold, disapproving tone.

Carys felt the weight of her hair tumbling round her shoulders and knew she looked as if she'd been ravaged to within an inch of her life. She was barefoot, half undressed, her lips bruised and swollen from the intensity of their passion, and her nipples thrust shamelessly against the cotton of her bra. Anyone looking at her would know precisely what she'd been doing.

She had a choice: an ignominious flight from the presidential suite looking like a complete wanton or a cosy *tête à tête* with Alessandro Mattani.

She was across the room before he could move a step.

'Just watch me.'

Alessandro stood on the private terrace of his suite, watching the dark-clad workers scurry across the bridge and swarm the streets. Morning peak hour and he'd already been at work for several hours.

Habitually he started early and finished late. But this morning…he raked a hand through his hair as frustration filled him.

He'd slept even less than usual, bedevilled by tantalising dreams of luscious pale limbs entwined with his, of generous feminine curves and silky smooth skin, of smoky blue-grey eyes enticing him to the brink of sexual fulfilment. Each time he'd woken, sweating, gasping for breath and formidably aroused, to the realisation Carys Wells had fled rather than allow them the release they both craved.

He rubbed a hand over his freshly shaved jaw, as if to dispel the tension there.

Even in sleep she denied him.

He could barely believe she'd run. Especially after he'd felt the hunger in her, a hunger as ravening as his own. It was a wonder their clothes hadn't disintegrated around them, their passion had been so combustible.

He grasped the iron balustrade savagely. Could it have been a tactic to tease him into wanting more then leave him aching with need? What could she hope to gain?

He shook his head. No woman was that good an actress. Besides, he knew every trick in the book when it came to conniving women, and Carys hadn't played the tease. He remembered the scent of her arousal, sharp and musky.

Oh, no, Carys Wells had wanted him all right.

Why had she denied them both?

A stiff breeze blew up from the river and chilled his skin. He should have taken things slower, scoped out the situation rather than allowing his driving need free rein.

One of the first things he'd learned when he entered the commercial world was to plan carefully and unemotionally and only strike at the most opportune moment.

Last night it hadn't been his brain doing the thinking.

He'd frightened her off. Her wide eyes had been desperate as she backed to the door. For an instant he'd even suspected they shone overbright.

A ripple of regret passed through him and he frowned.

His security team assured him she'd got home safely, unaware of their surveillance or their orders to keep her safe. Yet still Alessandro felt the weight of guilt. It was his fault she'd fled.

He should have controlled himself and conquered his animal instincts. Yet he'd been unable to comprehend anything but the need to possess her.

Alessandro scrubbed his palm over his face again, grimacing. He couldn't remember ever acting with less forethought. He'd been like a starving man set before a banquet, unable to summon even a shred of restraint.

Was he always like that with her?

The question tantalised him. The frustration of not knowing ate like acid into his gut.

He was so close, and still the answers eluded him.

A discreet ringtone interrupted his thoughts and he drew his cellphone from his pocket.

It was Bruno, head of his security team, reporting on Carys' movements this morning. Alessandro froze into immobility at the report, delivered in a carefully uninflected tone.

Eventually he roused himself enough to issue a few more orders. Then he took the phone from his ear and waited for the image Bruno was sending.

There it was. A little blurry with movement, but unmistakeable. Carys Wells, in a familiar dark suit and not a hair out of place. But what held Alessandro's attention wasn't his erstwhile lover. It was the burden she carried in her arms.

Small, rounded, riveting his attention.

A baby.

Carys had a child.

The air purged from Alessandro's lungs in a hiss of disbelief. His jaw tightened so hard his head began to throb as he stared at the image before him.

Whose child? The boyfriend from whom she'd been separated? Some other man? A long-term lover or a passing stranger?

Pain roused him from his turbulent thoughts. Alessandro looked down to discover he'd grasped the railing so hard the decorative ironwork had drawn blood on the fleshy part of his palm.

Dispassionately he stared at the welling redness, then back at the picture of Carys and her child.

Only then did Alessandro recognise the emotion surging so high it threatened to choke him. Fury. Raw sizzling wrath that she'd been with another man.

It didn't matter how or why they'd separated. Every instinct screamed that Carys belonged to *him*. Could it be any clearer after the way they'd been together? The intensity of their passion made every other liaison pale into insignificance.

He'd come seeking answers. Last night he'd discovered answers weren't enough. He wanted Carys too, for as long as the attraction between them held.

Looking at her holding another man's child in her arms sent spears of flame through his chest and gut.

The sight should have cured him of his lust.

Instead he felt a burning desire to discover the identity of the man who'd fathered Carys' baby and mash him into a pulp with his bare hands.

CHAPTER FOUR

CARYS pulled her long, flapping coat tight around herself as she left the staff entrance. A cheap second-hand purchase, it helped combat Melbourne's cold, but it was a size too large, billowing out in the wind and allowing chill draughts to tease her.

A glance at the louring sky made her pick up her pace, scurrying to avoid the blur of rain already washing over the city. With luck her train would be on time and she'd get home at a reasonable hour. Two of her colleagues had returned to work today, so she didn't have to stay back.

Carys looked forward to the luxury of some quiet time with Leo then a long luxurious soak and a good night's sleep.

Resolutely she avoided the knowledge that she'd probably spend another sleepless night tossing and turning.

She'd made it through the day in a state of numb shock, working like an automaton, except when the sight of a tall dark-haired man, or an unexpected call, froze the blood in her veins.

She'd expected him to come after her. If not last night when she'd left him high and dry, then today.

He knew where she worked. He knew far too much. Why had he left her alone?

Foreboding crept through her. He was biding his time.

It could only be Leo he wanted. Her precious boy. What else would drag Alessandro here from Italy?

The realisation was like a knife at her neck. A man with Alessandro's resources could get anything he wanted.

If he wanted Leo…

Carys had no illusions that he was here for anything else. For Alessandro, last night had simply been about the chance for hot sex.

Absence from his wife must be wearing on him.

Bile rose in Carys' throat, a savage, scouring bitterness. Shame flooded her and she ducked her head.

She hadn't even remembered he was tied to another woman! The overwhelming reality of his presence had blasted Carys back to a time when she'd been his, body and soul. When she'd believed he was hers. Before he had married his blue-blooded heiress.

Carys tasted salt on her tongue as she bit her lip.

Distress filled her at how close she'd come to compounding her stupidity in an act that would shatter her principles.

She hadn't been able to meet her eyes in the mirror this morning, recalling her uninhibited response to him.

Fury, disbelief and disappointment filled her. At him for using her as a convenience to assuage his physical needs. For not being the honourable man she'd once thought him. At herself for abandoning her pride and principles in letting him sweep her into his tempestuous embrace.

Carys squared her shoulders. She'd played the fool for the last time. Besides, he'd relinquished all rights when he—

A pair of massive mirror-polished black shoes blocked the pavement before her. Carys side-stepped to skirt the man, but with one long stride he moved too, forcing her to stop.

Her gaze climbed a pair of bulky legs in pin-striped trousers so beautifully tailored they almost tamed the rampantly muscled solidity of the man. Neat shirt, dark tie, perfectly fitting jacket and a swarthy face topped by pepper and salt hair. Gold winked in the man's earlobe as he turned his head and Carys stared, sure she'd seen him before.

'*Scusa, signorina.* This way, please.'

He extended one arm, gesturing towards the kerb.

Carys turned to see a limousine with tinted windows drawn up beside her, its back door open.

Her pulse sped up to thunder in her ears. A sprawl of long masculine limbs filled her vision of the interior and her heart rate spiked. The last thing she wanted was to share such an intimate space with Alessandro Mattani.

'You've got to be kidding,' she muttered, automatically stepping back from the road.

The large Italian moved closer, shepherding her towards the vehicle. Resolutely she planted her feet on the pavement, refusing to budge.

She looked around, hoping to find the street filled with people, but the few she saw were racing for cover as big fat drops of rain spattered the pavement. There was no one to interfere if Alessandro's goon tried to manhandle her into the car.

'Why don't you get in before you both get soaked?' asked a cool voice from the back of the limo.

Outraged dignity came to her rescue. 'And if I'd prefer to get drenched than share a car with you?'

'I'd say it was very selfish of you to force Bruno to suffer the same fate just for the sake of your pride.'

Her eyes rounded. Pride? Alessandro thought this was simply about pride?

The man beside her moved, closing in beside her, and Carys darted a glance at him, wondering if she had any hope of getting away. He was built like a rugby player, all dense-packed muscle. Right now he had that grim, blank-eyed set to his face that she'd seen on the super-tough minders of the rich and famous.

'Per favore, signorina.'

Drops splattered his jacket as the rain fell faster. He didn't bat an eyelid, just watched her with the stony countenance of a man ready to deal with anything.

She'd bet five feet six of female, hampered by heels and a skirt, would be the work of a moment to overpower.

'Don't let his looks fool you, Carys,' came a laconic voice from the limo's interior. 'Bruno has a weak chest. He's just got over a bout of bronchitis. I wouldn't like him to have a relapse. And you wouldn't want that on your conscience.'

Carys blinked, catching the merest flicker of expression on the security man's face. A smile? Surely not.

Movement to one side caught her eye, and she turned to find

Alessandro had slid to the edge of the seat and was regarding her with a peculiarly unreadable expression.

'His wife would flay me alive if I brought him home with pneumonia.'

Despite her anger, Carys felt her lips twitch. Once, long ago, Alessandro's dry wit had been one of the things that had drawn her to him. She'd almost forgotten that, her memories skewed by those final, unhappy days when banter and teasing had been absent between them.

'I would have thought blackmail was more your style,' she jeered. 'Or threats, rather than an appeal to my conscience.'

Rain trickled into her collar, but she stood ramrod straight. This man was dangerous.

A shrug of those lean shoulders and he said something in Italian that made Bruno move away to give them space. Carys barely had time to register the chance for escape when Alessandro's voice curled around her, silkily smooth. 'I regret last night, Carys. It wasn't planned.'

He paused, awaiting a response that she steadfastly refused to give. If that was his idea of an apology he had a lot to learn.

Alessandro's eyes narrowed as she stood rigid under his scrutiny. Something glittered in that forest-dark gaze that sent shivers of trepidation running through her. Despite his earlier light-hearted words, his stare sizzled. She guessed his deadpan expression disguised an anger almost as great as her own. Now she looked more closely, she read tension in his shoulders and grim mouth.

Too bad. She tilted her chin up, wishing she had a long aristocratic nose like his so she could look down it.

'But if that's the way you'd prefer to do this,' he purred, 'then I can oblige.'

She'd opened her mouth to say she preferred to have nothing to do with him, when his next words forestalled her.

'I'm sure the hotel management would be interested in the security camera footage of the lobby outside the presidential suite last night, and in the lift. If they cared to check the recording they'd find it…illuminating.'

'You wouldn't!' Shock hammered her like a physical blow, sucking out her breath. That tape would show her emerging from his suite in the early hours looking like…like…

'Wouldn't I?' His stare was unnervingly blank. 'I'm sure they frown on staff providing *personal* services to guests.' His tongue dripped with hateful innuendo and Carys burned with frustration and fury. Her hands clenched around the shoulder strap of her bag.

'I wasn't providing a service, you—'

'It doesn't matter what you were doing, Carys. All that matters is how the evidence appears.' He leaned back with a smug glimmer in his eyes.

Evidence. It sounded so formal.

It *would* be formal if anyone decided to check the recording. Formal enough to get her the sack.

Her heart dived and she shivered, but not from the rain's chill. She needed this job. How else could she support Leo? Good positions were hard to find for someone with limited qualifications.

Would Alessandro make good on his threat?

Once she'd thought she'd known this man. Had trusted him. Had even believed he was falling in love with her.

What a naïve innocent she'd been.

She'd learned the hard way not to trust her judgement with him. Better to assume him capable of anything to get his own way. He'd already made a fool of her once.

He was her enemy, threatening the life she'd begun to build, her independence, even, she feared, her child.

'What do you want?' She didn't care that her voice was scratchy with distress, despite her attempt to appear calm.

'To talk. We have unfinished business.'

He didn't wait for her to assent but slid back across the wide leather seat, making space for her.

Unfinished business.

That was how he described one little boy?

Her throat closed convulsively as the fight bled out of her. She couldn't ignore Alessandro. She had to face him and hope against hope she could retain some control of the situation.

She tottered forward on numb legs and entered the limousine, her wet coat sliding along a leather seat that looked and smelled fresh from the factory.

Only the best for the Conte Mattani.

Under no circumstances would she, an ordinary single mum with not an ounce of glamour, be classed as *the best*. Alessandro had made that abundantly clear in Italy.

Her heart bumped against her ribs. Had Alessandro decided her little boy was a different matter?

The limo door shut with a quiet click and she sagged back, shutting her eyes. She was cold to the bone.

There was no escape now.

Moments later the front door closed and the vehicle accelerated. Belatedly she remembered to do up her seatbelt. A swift sideways glance told her Alessandro wasn't happy, despite having got her where he wanted her.

The proud, spare lines of his face seemed austere and forbidding silhouetted against the city streets. He looked as approachable as some ancient king, brooding over judgement.

The flicker of unease inside her magnified into a hundred fluttering wings. She was at a disadvantage to him in so many ways.

His silence reinforced that she was here at his pleasure.

Carys flicked her gaze away, not deigning to ask where they were going. Two could play the silent game. It would give her time to marshal her resources.

As she stared straight ahead, trying to control her frantic, jumbled thoughts, she found herself looking through a smoky glass privacy-screen at the back of Bruno's head.

Recognition smote her.

'He was on my street. Last night!' Carys leaned forward to make sure. There was no mistaking the bunched-muscle silhouette of the minder's neck and shoulders, or the shape of his head.

As she'd walked up the ill-lit street to her block of flats in the early hours, she'd faltered, her heart skipping as she noticed a brawny man in jeans and a leather jacket just ahead. He looked to be waiting for someone. But as she'd hesitated he'd turned to stroll away in the opposite direction.

Nevertheless, she'd scurried inside as fast as possible. Her street was peaceful by day, but the shopping strip a few blocks away had been attracting unsavoury characters at night.

'Bruno, your bodyguard. He was outside my home.'

She swung round to find Alessandro watching her steadily. His lack of response infuriated her.

'You're not even bothering to deny it!'

'Why would I?' His brow furrowed in a hint of a frown that, annoyingly, didn't detract from his handsome looks.

'You had him follow me?' Already Alessandro had pried into her personnel records. Now his stooge had been scoping out her home. He had no qualms about invading her privacy.

'Of course.' He stared coolly as if wondering what the fuss was about. 'It was late. I had to make sure you got back all right.'

His explanation took the wind out of her sails and she slumped in her seat, her mind whirling.

'You were trying to *protect* me?'

Something indefinable flickered in his eyes. 'You were out alone at an hour when you should have been safely home.'

At least he didn't mention her state of disarray. Even in a pair of shoes borrowed from the staffroom, and with her shirt buttoned again, she'd felt as if the few people she'd met on her journey took one look and knew exactly what she'd been up to in the presidential suite.

Alessandro made her sound like a teenager in need of parental guidance. Not a twenty-five-year-old woman supporting herself and her son.

Yet it wasn't indignation Carys felt rise like a tide inside her. It was warmth, a furtive spark of pleasure, that he'd cared enough to worry about her safety.

In the old days she'd been thrilled by the way he'd looked after her, showing what she'd thought was a strongly protective nature.

Until she'd discovered her mistake. What she'd seen as caring had been his way of keeping her isolated, separate from the rest of his life. It had been a deliberate tactic to ensure she didn't know how he used her.

The lush melting warmth inside her dissipated as a chill blast of reality struck right to the bone.

'I'm perfectly capable of looking after myself! I was doing it long before you turned up.' Carys wrapped her arms around the faux-leather bag on her lap and turned away.

She was proud of what she'd achieved. When she'd arrived in Australia she'd been a mess, her heart in tatters, her confidence shattered. Even her destination of Melbourne was unplanned. She'd been too distraught to do more than turn up at the airport and board the first available flight home.

Now she'd built a new life for herself and Leo. She was working hard to achieve the financial security they needed.

'Is that so?' Scepticism dripped from each syllable as he held her with a glacial green stare. 'You really think that the best neighbourhood to bring up a child?'

Her fingers, busy fiddling with the zipper on her bag, froze. Every muscle tensed.

Now they'd come to the crux of the matter.

She waited for him to accuse her of being a bad mother, to demand his rights and push his case. Yet he remained silent, only his lowered brows hinting at displeasure.

'The flat is sunny and comfortable. And affordable.' It went against the grain to hint at her lack of funds, but no doubt he knew about her precarious finances.

Despite working right up till she went into labour, Carys had used all her meagre savings in the months after Leo's birth. If it hadn't been for the money her father had sent long-distance, she wouldn't have been able to support them. When the going had got really tough, she'd even thought of moving to be with her dad. Till she imagined his horror at the idea.

Only now, with her job at the Landford, could she make ends meet, though most of her wages went on childcare and rent and there was precious little for other necessities.

'And the location? Your neighbourhood is becoming a hub for drug dealing and prostitution.'

He didn't bother to hide his disapproval. If she hadn't been wearing a thick coat, his coruscating glare would have scraped off layers of skin.

'The reports are exaggerated,' she bluffed, refusing to admit he'd tapped into her own fear. That the cosy nest she'd created for her son grew less desirable by the week.

Only days ago there'd been more syringes found in the park and another bashing in the street. Carys had decided that, despite the friends she'd made locally, she'd look for somewhere else to bring up Leo.

'If you say so.' His tone implied boredom.

Carys was puzzled. This was his opportunity to weigh in with comments about her inability to care for Leo. To make a case that she shouldn't have sole custody.

Yet Alessandro seemed totally uninterested. Had she got it wrong? Hope rose shakily in her breast.

But if he wasn't here for her little boy, what did he want from her?

Alessandro tamped down the fury he'd felt ever since receiving this morning's report. Fury that Carys should live in such a neighbourhood. That she'd hooked up with a man who obviously refused to take care of her and her child.

That he, Alessandro, had let her get under his skin enough to be concerned for her!

He cursed himself for a fool. She'd walked out on him, moved on from whatever relationship they'd had. He should do the same. Dignity and pride demanded it.

He *would*, he vowed, once he knew all he needed to about those blank months.

Yet that sense of intimate connection still hammered at him. It was stronger even than the cool logic around which he built his life.

Despite her antipathy and her child by another man, Alessandro couldn't banish the possessiveness that swamped him when he was with her. It consumed him.

Never had he experienced such feelings.

His fists tightened as his temples throbbed. Flickers of images taunted him. Whether remnants of last night's erotic dreams or snippets of memory, he didn't know.

He wanted to hate her for the unaccustomed weakness she wrought in him. Yet the bruised violet smudges under her eyes snagged his attention. It had taken more than one sleepless night to put them there.

His belly clenched as he took in her pallor and the way her worn coat dwarfed her. Last night he'd seen she was tired, but he'd been too overwhelmed by his own cataclysmic response to register what looked now like utter exhaustion.

He'd been impatient to solve the riddle that had haunted him so long. Too busy losing himself in her lush curves and feminine promise to admit the extent of her vulnerability.

That vulnerability clawed at his conscience. He should never have unleashed the beast of sexual hunger that roared into life when she was near.

'Where's this boyfriend of yours? Why doesn't he help you?' He snapped the words out, surprising himself. It wasn't his way to blurt his thoughts.

Wary eyes met his. They darkened like storm clouds and instinctively he knew she concealed something.

Carys blinked and looked away. 'I'm fine by myself. I don't need anyone to—'

'Of course you do. You shouldn't be living in this area. Not with a baby.' He spared the run-down neighbourhood the briefest of glances. It was seedy, an area of urban decline. 'He should help you.'

Her mouth remained mutinously closed.

Alessandro knew a wholly uncharacteristic desire for hot-blooded argument. He, who never let anything ruffle his equanimity! Who was a master at sublimating useless emotions and pursuing his goals with single-minded purpose.

How this woman unsettled him. The last twenty-four hours had been a roller coaster of unfamiliar feelings that made a mockery of his habitual control.

He resented that more than anything.

'Who is he, Carys? Why do you protect him?'   .

Because she loved him? Alessandro's mouth flattened. This should be none of his business, yet he couldn't let go.

'I'm not protecting anyone!' she muttered. 'There's no one. What I told you—'

'You said you'd argued. That's no excuse for him walking out on his child and its mother.'

Alessandro's nostrils filled with pungent distaste. His reaction to the idea of any man getting Carys pregnant was bone-deep rage. His belly cramped as he strove to master his feelings.

Who *was* this woman that she made him react so?

She stared silently, an arrested expression on her face.

'Is he someone you work with?' The words shot out through gritted teeth.

She shook her head. 'Don't be absurd.'

There was nothing absurd about it. Working side by side led too easily to intimacy. He'd had to move his PA elsewhere after she'd mistaken their working relationship for something else. He'd lost count of the female employees and business associates who'd thought work the perfect way into his bed.

Silently he cursed himself for needing to know.

'He's married? Is that it?'

Carys stared into his glowering face and struggled against a sense of unreality. He looked genuinely perplexed. Deep grooves bracketed a mouth that morphed from sensual perfection into a wrathful line.

She shook her head as if to clear it. She mustn't have heard right.

'There *is* no man in my life.' She hesitated, knowing a craven urge to avoid the truth. 'I made that up so you'd leave me alone.'

Alessandro's brow furrowed, his eyebrows disapproving black slashes that tilted down in the centre. And still he looked better than any man she knew.

'Don't deny it. Of course there's a man.'

'Are you calling me a liar?' His refusal to accept her word reopened a wound that had never healed. He hadn't believed her before. Why should things be different now? Her word wasn't good enough.

Pain mixed with Carys' fury. Her distress was all the more potent for having been suppressed so long.

'Spare me the show of innocence,' he sneered. 'You didn't get pregnant all by yourself. Or are you trying to tell me it was an immaculate conception?'

'You bastard!' Her arm shot out faster than thought. An instant later her hand snapped across his cheek as her fury finally boiled over.

Her palm tingled. Her whole arm trembled with the force of the slap. Her breath came in hard, shallow pants. She barely noticed the dangerous glint in his narrowing eyes or the way he loomed closer.

Then, out of the blue, the implication of his words sank in. Relief swamped her, making her shake as she sagged back in her seat.

He wasn't here to take Leo away.

Hysterical laughter swelled inside at her stupidity. Alessandro didn't want to take her boy. Of course he didn't! He'd made his disinterest and disapproval clear from the start. He'd left her in no doubt both she and her baby weren't good enough for him and his rarefied circle of moneyed friends.

Why had she thought he'd changed? Because part of her still foolishly ached to believe he was the fantasy man she'd fallen in love with?

Pain welled.

It felt as if Alessandro had taken her last precious fragment of hope and callously ground it underfoot, shattering a fragile part of her.

'You really are some piece of work, Alessandro Mattani.' Her voice was hoarse with distress, her throat raw with pain as if she'd swallowed broken glass. 'I should have known you hadn't changed.'

'Me, change?' Astonishment coloured his voice, at odds with his look of rigid control.

'Yes, you. You coward.' Carys pressed a palm to her stomach, trying to prevent the churn of nausea. 'Even after all this time you refuse to acknowledge your own son.'

CHAPTER FIVE

THE woman was mad.

Or conniving.

Alessandro met her glittering eyes, dark now as a thunder storm, and saw lightning flash.

Did she even notice that he'd grabbed her wrist and yanked it from his face? That he still held it in an implacable grip?

She didn't seem to notice anything except her own fury.

His cheek burned from her slap and pride demanded instant retribution. No one, man or woman, insulted Alessandro Mattani.

Yet he held himself in check. He would not resort to violence against a woman.

More importantly, he needed to know what she was up to, this mad woman with the wild accusations and glorious eyes.

'Don't be absurd. I don't have a child.' That was one thing he'd never forget, no matter how severe his injuries.

Besides, he'd always taken care not to lay himself open to paternity claims. He enjoyed short-term liaisons, but that didn't mean he took risks with his health or his family honour.

'Spare me the act, Alessandro,' she hissed. 'Others might be impressed, but I'm not. I gave up being impressed the day I left you.'

He frowned as he felt tremors rack her body and her pulse catapult into overdrive.

'You're angry because our relationship ended?'

Women never liked knowing they held a temporary place in his life. Too often they set their sights on becoming the Contessa

Mattani. But he had no illusions about matrimony. For him it would be a duty, to carry on the family name. A duty he was happy to postpone.

Her mouth opened in a short, humourless laugh. 'I wouldn't have stayed if you'd paid me,' she spat out. 'Not once I knew what you were really like.'

Such vehemence, such hatred, was new to Alessandro. The shock of it ran through him like a jolt of electricity. It felt as if he held a jumping live wire in his hand, liable to twist unpredictably at any moment and burn him to cinders.

She was unlike anything or anyone in his well-ordered life. *She fascinated him.*

'What's this about a child?' *That* sort of claim was one he would never take lightly.

Her mouth twisted in a grimace. 'Forget it,' she muttered, turning her head away. Her dismissive tone would anger a less controlled man.

Carys tried to tug her hand free, but he held her easily. He had no intention of letting her take another swipe at him. Swiftly he captured her other hand, holding both effortlessly till she gave up trying to escape and subsided, chest heaving, against the back of the seat.

'I can hardly forget it.' He pulled her hands, making her turn. Studiously he ignored the way her rapid breathing emphasised the swell of her breasts. 'Tell me.'

Thick dark lashes rose to reveal silvery-blue eyes that flashed with repressed emotion. Her pulse pounded beneath his fingers and she swiped the tip of her tongue over her lips as if to moisten them.

Instantly desire flared in his belly. *Just like that.*

The immediacy of his response would have stunned him if he hadn't experienced it last night. Whatever the secret of her feminine allure, he responded to it with every particle of testosterone in his body.

He watched her hesitate and kept his expression unreadable. All the while he was aware of the way her moist pink lips unconsciously invited him to plunder her mouth. His fingers tightened on her hands, as if ready to tug her close.

'There's nothing to tell.' Her look was pure belligerence. 'You have a child. But you already know that.' She paused; for the first time the heat in her expression disappeared and her eyes turned glacial, stabbing him with invisible icy shards. 'Why make me repeat what you know?'

'I want the truth. Is that too much to ask?' Finally anger exploded behind Alessandro's façade of calm. A roaring flame of wrath at this woman who turned his life inside out. He strove to resist shaking the truth out of her.

He couldn't remember ever being so irate.

But then no woman had ever dared make such accusations. Plus the frustration of not knowing his own past would drive any man wild. Alessandro abhorred that sneaking sense of powerlessness, not remembering.

Her chin lifted. 'Is it too much to ask that you stop crushing my hands?'

Instantly he released her, flexing fingers rigid with tension. He hadn't intended to hurt her. Another disturbing sign that his control was close to shattering.

'Thank you.' She paused, her gaze skating sideways. 'I promise not to slap you again. That was…unintentional.' She turned. 'We're here.' She spoke quickly, relief evident in every syllable.

Already Bruno was opening the door to the pavement. The driver stood at Alessandro's door, waiting for him to alight.

'We'll finish this discussion inside.'

'I'm not sure I want you in my home,' she countered.

'You think I *want* to be there?' Being with Carys opened a Pandora's Box of conflicting feelings he could do without.

But he needed to fill the gaps and banish once and for all the nagging sense of something missing in his life. Besides, he had to end this nonsense about fathering a child. He would not countenance such allegations.

Alessandro unfolded his legs from the car and stood up. He felt stiff, as if his muscles had cramped during the drive. He pushed his shoulders back and looked around the street. Graffiti marred the building opposite and a couple of ground-floor windows were boarded up further down the block.

Carys scurried ahead into an ugly square building, not looking back. Her shoulders were hunched and her head bent.

But she couldn't avoid him. He stepped forward.

'Signor Conte.' Bruno waited on the pavement for him.

'Yes?' Alessandro paused, his eyes on Carys.

'On the way here I received answers to the enquiries I made this morning. I didn't like to interrupt your discussion with *la signorina.*'

Bruno's careful tone snared Alessandro's attention, dragging it from his furious thoughts. He turned to meet his security chief's blank stare, sensing he wouldn't like this.

'And?'

'There's no record of a marriage. Signorina Wells is single.'

So, she hadn't bothered to marry the baby's father.

Alessandro shoved his hands deep into his pockets, refusing to examine the emotions stirring at that news.

'There's more?'

Bruno nodded. 'The birth was just over a year ago here in Melbourne.' There wasn't a hint of expression in his voice and a tickle of premonition feathered Alessandro's spine.

'What other details did you get?'

'The mother is given as Carys Antoinette Wells, receptionist, of this address.' Bruno gestured to the tired red-brick block of flats.

Alessandro waited, instinct making his skin crawl. 'And the rest?'

Bruno's eyes flickered away. He drew himself up straighter. 'The father is listed as Alessandro Leonardo Daniele Mattani of Como, Italy.'

Despite the fact that by now he'd half expected it, each word slammed into Alessandro's gut with the force of a sledgehammer.

His name. His identity.

His honour.

Damn her for using him in this way! She'd taken his name and dragged it in the mud with her petty manipulations.

What did she hope to achieve? Money? Position? A hint of respectability even though her child was born out of wedlock?

But why hadn't she come forward if she'd wanted to try screwing cash from him? Was she waiting for the most auspicious time to approach him?

As if there would ever be a good time for such a plan!

He felt his lips stretch in a grimace of distaste that bared his teeth. His nostrils flared and the blood pounded loud and fast in his ears.

'Wait here,' he barked. Without waiting for a response, he strode up the cement pavement to the eyesore of a building. A red mist hazed his vision. The need for justice, for retribution, spurred him on.

This was about far more now than curiosity. More even than the stirring of a libido that had been dormant since he'd woken in hospital twenty-two months ago.

Carys Wells had gone too far. She'd sullied his honour.

For that she would pay.

Carys had only just collected Leo from next door and put him down, still sleeping.

The rap on her door came too soon. She looked at Leo's peaceful form and felt a tug of intense protectiveness. There'd been no time to decide how to deal with Alessandro.

Who was she kidding? She'd always been putty in his hands. Even now when she almost hated him, she had no illusions about that.

She'd never be rid of him until they had this out.

Reluctantly she walked through the miniscule flat, wiping her damp hands on her skirt. Her legs shook as another tattoo of raps sounded.

The glorious surge of anger had seeped away, leaving her prey to nerves and bone-melting exhaustion.

Fumbling, she unlatched the door and swung it wide.

Alessandro stood there, vibrating with a dangerous energy that wrapped right round her, squeezing her lungs. His eyes sizzled with a fury she'd seen only once before. The day he'd told her, with arctic composure, she'd outstayed her welcome.

Yet even now his potent charisma tugged at her. She bit down hard on her lip, desperate for the strength to face him.

Wordlessly he strode past her into the small sitting room-cum-kitchen. For such a big man he still managed to avoid brushing against her which, given the size of the entry, was a feat in itself.

Her lips turned up in a grimace as she pushed the door shut. He couldn't bear to touch her now she'd called him on his behaviour. How different from last night when his hands had been all over her, marking her with his own special brand of sensual possession.

Hot shame suffused her.

'You used my name for your bastard child.'

She spun round to find him towering over her, the image of disdain. But his anger was no match for hers.

'Don't ever talk about him like that!' She ignored the blast of his disapproval and jabbed an accusing finger.

'What? You're telling me you married after all?'

'No! Why would I go looking for a husband after my child's father had already rejected us?'

Alessandro leaned forward, using his superior height to intimidate her. 'For the same reason you perjured yourself, listing me as the father on the birth certificate. To try to claim some measure of respectability. Or financial support.'

The irony of his accusation hit her full force. If she'd expected support of any kind from Alessandro she'd been grossly mistaken.

She might have harboured a fatal weakness for this overbearing, arrogant, gorgeous man, but, where her son was concerned, she refused to be bullied. She stuck her hands on her hips and stared back, glare for glare.

'It was for Leo. He has a right to know who his father is.'

'Have you no shame?' Alessandro's dark green eyes sliced right through her self-possession.

'Only about the fact that I was once foolish enough to…' She stopped herself in time. She would not lay herself open to derision by admitting the feelings she'd once held for him. 'To believe in you.'

But she sensed he wasn't listening. He was absorbed in his own thoughts.

'Leo? You called him—'

'Leonardo. After your father.' She hesitated, aware now of her sentimental folly in choosing a family name for her son. She'd wanted to give him a link to his paternal family, even though that family had roundly rejected him.

Had she secretly thought one day Alessandro might be pleased to have the baby named after the father he'd lost? How misguided she'd been. He looked as she imagined some aristocrat of old must have when confronted with a troublesome serf.

'You dared to—'

'I'm not ashamed of what I did,' she bit out between clenched teeth. 'Live with it, Alessandro!'

A muffled wail sounded. Immediately Carys spun round and hurried to the bedroom she shared with Leo. She refused to stay and be reviled by Alessandro Mattani of all men.

Moments later Leo was in her arms, a warm cuddly bundle smelling of baby powder and sunshine and little boy. Carys held him against her and shut her eyes, feeling the serenity and joy she always experienced holding him.

'Mumum!' He reached up and patted her face.

Carys nuzzled his soft cheek then held him away. 'Hello, sweetie. Did you have a good day?'

His face split in a broad smile. 'Mum!' Then something over her shoulder caught his attention and he stared, his grin fading.

The skin on her neck prickled as she sensed Alessandro's presence in the room. She didn't have to turn to know he stood behind her.

She froze.

For so long she'd daydreamed about him coming to find her and Leo. He'd admit he'd been wrong and be devastated by the pain he'd caused. Carys would even find it in her heart to forgive him once she realised his true feelings for her and changed his ways. He'd take one look at Leo and his heart would melt like hers had when she'd first seen her son.

But that would never be.

There was no warmth in his heart for either of them.

Apprehension trickled like hot ice down her backbone. She couldn't bear it if he took out his anger on Leo. She cuddled her son tighter, but he leaned sideways, craning to keep Alessandro in view.

'Mumum!'

'No, darling. Not mummy.' For a split second she knew a hysterical urge to tell him it was daddy. But she wouldn't invite Alessandro's wrath.

She turned, shoulders braced and chin up, holding her baby close. If Alessandro dared make one more disparaging remark—

But she needn't have worried. All trace of arrogance and anger had vanished. Instead her tormentor stood curiously still, arms loose at his sides. His brows were knitted and he stared at Leo as if he'd never seen a baby before.

Instinctively Carys cuddled her son nearer. She smoothed back his glossy dark hair, almost long enough to be cut. But Leo paid her no heed. He was busy gazing up at the man who refused to be called his father.

She remembered how Alessandro's collar-length hair had once been like sable under her hands, just like Leo's. Their eyes were the same too. Though Leo's reminded her of a cheeky pixie's, with their twinkle, and Alessandro's showed no warmth at all. They might have been made of rock crystal.

She watched Alessandro's hands clench. The tendons in his neck stretched taut.

And still he stared at Leo.

A shiver raced down her spine.

'How old is he?' Alessandro's voice was curiously husky.

'He had his first birthday six weeks ago.'

'He was born early?'

'No. He went to full term.' Why all the questions?

Leo's sudden movement took her by surprise. He wriggled in her arms and lunged forward with all his weight as if trying to swim across the gap between himself and Alessandro.

'Mumum!' His hands opened and closed as if trying to grasp the big man before him. But Alessandro didn't move.

Carys felt her heart spasm at the sight of her little boy reaching for his father. He was doomed to disappointment.

Alessandro would never acknowledge him.

Would never love him. Or her.

Finally, after all this time, she shrugged off the last tarnished remnants of hope. The ache in her throat nearly choked her, but she felt freer than she had in almost two years. Surely, in time, the wounds would heal.

Meanwhile she had to protect Leo from the pain of knowing his dad didn't want him. She'd make up for the lack of a father, she decided fiercely. Leo would never want for love or encouragement or kindness. Not like she had.

Her arms tightened and he wailed, turning accusing eyes on her. 'Mum!'

'Yes, sweetheart. I'm sorry. Are you hungry? Are you ready for something to eat?' She took a step towards the door, studiously ignoring the tall man, standing as if riveted to the spot. 'Let's get you some food, shall we?'

It seemed a lifetime before Alessandro moved. Finally he stepped aside. 'After you.'

Carys didn't deign to respond.

She'd made it to the kitchen, Leo clamped safely on her hip, when a deep voice halted her in her tracks.

'Tell me how you came to be pregnant.'

He had to be kidding!

She whirled round to find him only a metre away, his eyes glued to her son. The intensity of his gaze unnerved her and she stroked her palm protectively over Leo's cheek.

'Oh, come *on*, Alessandro!' Her lips were stiff with fury. 'I don't know what sort of game you're playing, but I've had enough. This stops now.'

Dark green eyes lifted to pinion hers. Banked heat flared in that hooded gaze. Instantly a coil of reaction twisted in the pit of her stomach. Fear and something else she refused to name.

'No, Carys.' His words fell like blows, slow and heavy. 'It's just starting.'

Abruptly he turned to pace the room, but not before she read the bleak emptiness in his eyes.

'Because as far as I know for certain, we met for the first time last night.'

CHAPTER SIX

'SO THAT'S it? We met in the Alps, where you had a job in a ski resort. We had an affair and I invited you back to my home.' Alessandro kept his voice neutral, as emotionless as if he were reading a company report rather than repeating the most astonishing thing he'd heard in years.

The whole idea was absurd.

He'd never invited any woman to share his home. The only woman he could imagine living there was the woman he'd one day make his wife. A woman he hadn't yet met.

He'd spent his adult years ensuring the women he dated understood he wasn't interested in deep, meaningful relationships. That was just female-speak for snaring a rich man gullible enough to believe she wanted him for his character and personality!

'We lived together, but it didn't work out, and you came back to Australia,' he continued, watching her avoid his gaze. 'You discovered you were pregnant and you called my home repeatedly, eventually spoke to my stepmother and as a result, believed I wanted nothing further to do with you?'

'That's about the size of it.'

Her offhand response fuelled the remnants of his earlier temper. Didn't she realise how vital this was?

Alessandro's fists clenched tight. He abhorred the need to share the fact of his memory loss with a stranger. Even a stranger with whom he'd once been intimate.

He'd been brought up never to show vulnerability, never to

feel it. No wonder his discomfort now was marrow deep. His certainties, his sense of order, his grasp of the situation were far too shaky for a man accustomed to taking charge.

Still Carys didn't look at him but busied herself feeding the tot in the high chair. Was it his imagination or was she taking far too long fussing with cloths and dishes?

Alessandro kept his eyes on her, rather than her son. Meeting those big green eyes so like his own made him uneasy. And the way the boy kept staring at him, surely that wasn't normal.

The child wasn't his. He'd *know* if he had a son.

He'd always been careful about contraception. He would have children at the appropriate time, when he'd found a suitable bride. She'd be clever, chic, at home in his world, sexy. She wouldn't bore him after two weeks as most females did.

The harsh overhead light caught rich colour as Carys bent her head and the child tugged a lock of burnished hair loose from her prim bun.

Something snagged in Alessandro's chest, looking at her. And her son.

No!

He refused to feel anything except annoyance that her story didn't trigger any memories. It was all still an infuriating blank.

She turned and lifted the baby high in her arms, her prim white blouse dragging taut with the movement.

Something plunged in the pit of Alessandro's belly and heat spread in his lower body.

At least one thing was explained: his sense of possessiveness when he looked at Carys. She'd been his and, if her story was true, they'd shared a relationship unlike his usual liaisons. He'd desired her enough, trusted her enough, to install her in his own home.

Incredible! Yet it would be easy to check.

Had he planned to keep her as a long-term mistress? The idea fascinated him.

Watching the tight material of her skirt mould her thighs, the thin cotton of her blouse stretch over her breasts, the idea didn't seem quite as absurd as it should.

If it weren't for the baby, he'd be tempted to take up right now where they'd left off last night.

Sudden pain slashed behind his eyes and through his temple as he struggled to remember. The headache he'd fought in the car hovered. He was well now. Recovered. Only occasionally did the pain recur, a reminder of the past.

'Are you all right?' Smoky eyes held his. He dropped his hand from his temple and stretched his legs in front of him, shifting his weight on the lumpy sofa.

'Perfectly.' He paused, following the movement of a chubby little starfish hand that patted her breast then tugged at one of her buttons. A moment later she caught the baby's hand in hers.

Alessandro raised his eyes. Her cheeks were delicately flushed, her lips barely parted.

'You haven't told me why we split up.'

The colour in her cheeks intensified. But not, he'd swear, with sexual awareness. Her nostrils pinched, and her lips firmed.

'I don't want to talk about this. There's no point.'

'Humour me,' he murmured, leaning forward.

He wanted his pound of flesh. But what choice did she have? He looked as immovable as Uluru. Instinctively she knew he wouldn't leave till his curiosity was satisfied.

Carys believed him about his missing memory. He looked so uncomfortable she knew it was a truth he didn't want to share. She'd heard of such amnesia from her medico eldest brother. And it explained so much that had puzzled her. Like why Alessandro had come round the globe to find her.

What other reason could he have for going to such lengths? Especially since he'd dumped her so unceremoniously.

She bit her lip, glad she was the only one to remember every ignominious detail of that scene.

'You don't remember *anything?*' Pointless to ask, given his patent lack of knowledge about her, about them. Yet it seemed impossible she'd been wiped totally from his memory.

Once they'd been close. Not just physically intimate, but close as soulmates, or so it had seemed.

How could all that just disappear completely?

Because what they'd shared was far less important to Alessandro than it had been to her?

'My memory stops several months before my father's death.' His words were terse. She guessed he viewed amnesia as a weakness he should be able to master. 'I don't remember meeting you.' His tone implied he still doubted what she'd told him. 'Those months are blank. I don't even remember driving before the accident. Just waking up in hospital.'

Slowly Carys lowered herself into the rocking chair. She let Leo stand on her thighs while she held his hands. It was a game he loved, marching on the spot.

Besides, it gave her a chance to rest her shaky legs. The shock of Alessandro's revelations was a stunning blow. She still felt faintly nauseous and her limbs trembled, thinking of him injured seriously enough to cause amnesia.

'You didn't tell me how the accident happened.' She paused, wondering if her concern was too obvious. But she had to know. She avoided staring at the scar reaching up to his temple. Instead she fixed her attention on a spot over his shoulder.

His shrug was fluid and easy.

'I was driving to Milan. The car skidded in the wet when I swerved to avoid a driver on the wrong side of the road.'

On the way to the office, then. Of course. He preferred to drive himself, claiming it helped him sort out his priorities for the day's business. From the rough timeline he'd mentioned, it must have happened soon after she left.

Had she thought, even for an instant, that her departure would disrupt his precious business schedule?

Her ridiculous naivety still stunned her.

'And you're all right?' Her heart pounded, imagining the scene. Carys swallowed hard on a jagged splinter of regret and fear. 'No other after-effects? No pain?'

No matter what she told herself, she hadn't completely severed her feelings for this man. She should despise him for the way he'd treated her, yet her conflicting emotions weren't so straightforward.

Carys refused to meet his intent gaze, choosing instead to watch Leo as he babbled to her.

'I'm perfectly healthy.'

Alessandro paused so long she looked up. He stared straight into her eyes as if reading her hunger for every detail. Her need for reassurance. Eventually he continued, his clipped words indicating how little he cared to dwell on his injuries.

'I was lucky. I had lacerations and a couple of fractures.'

At her hissed indrawn breath he shrugged. 'I mended quickly. I was only in hospital a few weeks. The main concern was my memory loss.' Darkening eyes bored into hers. 'But the specialists say there's nothing I can do about that except let nature take its course. There's no other brain damage.'

Carys slumped back, only now acknowledging the full depth of her fears. Relief warred with a sense of unreality.

'I see.' This strange, constrained conversation didn't seem real given the past they shared. But it gave Carys a little time to work through the implications of his news.

He mightn't remember her, but last night in his suite he'd seduced her with a combustible passion that had sheared straight through every defence she'd painstakingly erected in the last two years.

How had he done that if he couldn't even recall her?

Was he such an awesome lover he could make any woman feel the heady, mind-blowing certainty that she wanted nothing more than Alessandro Mattani, unbridled and consummately masculine? Were the intimacies she'd shared with him and always thought so special, the wondrous sensations, something he shared with countless women?

Her weakness mortified her.

'And your wife?' Carys failed to keep the bitterness from her voice as she choked out the word. 'I assume she's not with you?'

'Wife?' The single syllable slashed through the heavy atmosphere in the room. 'You're not saying I have a wife?'

Did she imagine it or had he paled? His lazy sprawl morphed into stark rigidity as he sat up, staring.

Carys hesitated. 'You were single when I left, but you were

seeing someone else, planning to marry her. Principessa Carlotta.' She couldn't prevent distaste colouring her voice.

Of course Alessandro would only marry one of his own, a rich, privileged aristocrat.

Carys swallowed bile as memories surged. Of how she'd obstinately disregarded his stepmother's warnings about Alessandro's intentions. And about her true, temporary place in his world. Of how she'd foolishly pinned her belief and hopes on the tender passionate words he whispered in her ear. On the rapture of being with him, being loved by him.

No! Having sex with him. The love had been all on her side.

'You seem to imply I did more than just *see* her.' His tone was outraged; his eyes flashed a furious warning. 'And that I did so while you and I were…together.'

If the cap fits, buddy. 'So you did.' Deliberately she turned away to focus on Leo, happily jouncing on her knees.

'You're mistaken.' Alessandro didn't raise his voice, but his whisper was lethally quiet, an unmistakeable warning. 'I would never stoop to such despicable behaviour.' Green eyes clashed with hers. They were so vibrant with indignation she expected to see sparks shoot from their depths.

'I was there, remember.' Carys took a slow breath, forcing down the rabid, useless jealousy that even now clawed to the surface. She concentrated on keeping her voice even. 'And unlike you I have perfect recall.'

Silence. His stare would have stripped paint at twenty paces. It scoured her mercilessly.

Yet Carys refused to back down. He might believe he was incapable of such behaviour, but if his memory ever returned he was doomed to disillusionment.

'I don't need to remember to know the truth, Carys.' He leaned forward, all semblance of relaxation gone. His voice echoed an unshakeable certainty. 'No matter what you think you understand about that time, I would never betray one lover with another. Never have two lovers at the same time. It wouldn't be honourable.'

Not honourable!

Carys suppressed an anguished laugh.

Was it honourable to have a lover share his bed but exclude her from the rest of his life because she wasn't good enough for his aristocratic friends? To use her for temporary sex while he courted another woman?

Whatever had gone wrong between Alessandro and the *principessa* to prevent the marriage, that was exactly what he'd been up to.

Carys had simply been convenient, gullible, expendable.

She swung her head away, refusing to look at him. Even now the pain was too raw. A cold, leaden lump rose in her throat, but she refused to reveal her vulnerability.

She drew a slow breath. 'When I tried to contact you about the pregnancy, your stepmother said you were preparing for your wedding. She made it clear you had no time to spare for an ex-mistress.'

'Livia said that?' His astonished tone drew her unwilling gaze. His eyebrows jammed together in a V of puzzlement. 'I can't believe it.'

No. That was the problem. He hadn't believed her before either. Her word meant nothing against his suspicions. The reminder stiffened her backbone.

'Frankly, Alessandro, I don't care what you believe.'

'It's true Livia is fond of Carlotta,' he murmured as if to himself. 'And that she wants me to marry. But arranging a wedding? It never went that far.'

How convenient his loss of memory was.

Carys had confirmation of the betrothal from another source too. But most convincing of all had been the sight of Alessandro with the glamorous, blue-blooded Carlotta. Even now the recollection stabbed, sharp as a twisting stiletto in her abdomen, making her hunch involuntarily.

The princess had stared up at him with exactly the same besotted expression Carys knew she herself had worn since the day he'd swept her off her feet and into his bed. Alessandro had kept the other woman close, his arm protectively around her as if she were made of delicate porcelain. He'd gazed into her eyes, utterly absorbed in their intimate conversation as if she were the only woman in the world.

As if he didn't have a convenient lover waiting obediently at home for him.

Carys blinked to banish the heat glazing the back of her eyes. Resolutely she focused instead on Livia's dismissive words when Carys had rung to tell Alessandro about her pregnancy.

Alessandro will do what is necessary to provide for the child if it's his. But don't expect him to contact you in person. Her tone had made it clear Carys was too socially inferior to warrant anything more than a settlement engineered by his formidable legal team. *The past is the past. And questions about your, shall we say…extra-curricular activities raise suspicions about the identity of the child's father.*

That slur, above all, had been hard to swallow.

How furious Alessandro's stepmother would have been if she'd known Carys hadn't accepted her word. Instead she'd left numerous messages on Alessandro's private phone and sent emails, even a hand-written letter. She'd been so desperate for personal contact.

Only after months of deliberate, deafening silence had she finally accepted he wanted nothing to do with either her or her unborn child. Then she'd determined to turn her back on the past and start afresh, not even considering a legal bid to win child support. Leo was better off without a father like that.

Yet now it seemed Alessandro hadn't known about her pregnancy.

Her breath jammed in her throat. All this time he hadn't known! He hadn't rejected Leo at all.

Nor was he married.

Her head spun, trying to take in the implications, her emotions a whirling jumble. Once she might have believed that would change everything.

Now she knew better.

One glance at Alessandro confirmed it. He was absorbed in his thoughts, totally oblivious to the little boy perched on her lap, twisting around time and again to try catching the attention of the big man who so effortlessly dominated their flat.

Alessandro had no interest in her either. She was nothing but a source of information.

Or an easy lay.

A shudder passed through her as memories of last night's passion stirred. Carys stiffened her resolve.

She looked into her baby's excited green gaze. He twinkled back at her mischievously as he nattered away in a language all his own. *He* was the important thing in her life. Not ancient dreams of happily ever after with the wrong man.

Whether Alessandro had known about the pregnancy or not didn't matter. What mattered was that the grand passion they'd shared had been a cheap affair, not a love on which to build a future. And he couldn't have made it clearer he had no interest in Leo.

Bridges burned. End of story.

Carys ignored the ache welling deep inside at the finality of it all and summoned a wobbly smile for Leo.

'Time for a bath, young man.' She gathered him close and stood on creaky legs. Suddenly she felt old beyond her years. Old with grief for what her son would never have, and with a stupid, obstinate hurt at being rejected again. After a lifetime of not measuring up, not being quite good enough, it was stupid to feel so wounded, but there it was.

'Why did I tell you to leave my home? You still haven't told me.'

She looked across to see Alessandro on his feet, hands jammed deep in his trouser pockets. He stood as far from her as he could while remaining in the same room.

Didn't that say it all?

'I'd decided to go anyway.' She lifted her chin. After learning about Alessandro and Carlotta the scales had fallen from her eyes. Carys knew she had to get as far away from him as she could. 'But you accused me of having an affair, of betraying your trust.'

The irony should have been laughable. But Carys had never felt less like laughing. She jiggled Leo higher in her weary arms and straightened her back.

'An affair? With whom?' His brows furrowed and his features took on a remote, hawk-like cast. Condemnation radiated from him.

'With Stefano Manzoni. He's—'

'I know who he is.' If anything, Alessandro's scowl deepened. His jaw set like stone and a pulse worked in his temple.

'Nice company you keep,' he said after a moment, his voice coolly disapproving.

Talk about double standards!

Carys jerked her chin higher. 'I thought he *was* nice. At first.' Until he wouldn't take no for an answer. He was another macho Italian male who couldn't cope with rejection. Though, to be fair, she'd never felt unsafe with Alessandro. 'I would have thought that as your Princess Carlotta's cousin he'd be utterly respectable.'

'She's not *my* Carlotta.' The words emerged through taut lips.

'Whatever.' Carys hunched stiff shoulders. 'Now, it's time for me to bathe Leo.' Her composure was in tatters and her limbs trembled with exhaustion. She felt like a wrung-out dishrag. 'I'd appreciate it if you'd go now.' She couldn't take any more.

Alessandro's appearance had dredged up emotions she thought she'd vanquished. Emotions that threatened to undo her. She needed desperately to be alone.

All she had left was the torn remnants of her pride, and Carys refused to collapse in a heap while he was here.

Head high, she walked on unsteady legs towards the front door, intending to show him out.

Leo's sudden sideways dive out of her arms took her completely unawares. One minute she was holding him. The next he was plunging headlong towards the floor when his bid to throw himself at Alessandro failed.

'Leo!'

Belatedly Carys grabbed for him, her weariness banished as adrenaline pumped hard and fast through her bloodstream, but her reactions were too slow.

'It's all right. I've got him.' How Alessandro got there so fast she didn't know, but he scooped Leo up in his arms just before he hit the floor.

Her heart catapulted against her ribs, slowing only when she saw he had the baby safe in his large hands. Relief shook her so hard her legs wobbled.

He held Leo awkwardly, at a distance from himself.

As if he couldn't bear to touch him? Or as a man would who'd never had experience with babies?

Carys hesitated, trying to decide which. In that moment Leo latched onto Alessandro's suit-clad arm, plucking at the fabric as if trying to climb closer. Green eyes met green, and Leo frowned, his chubby face puckering as he regarded the unsmiling man before him.

Finally, like the sun emerging from behind a cloud, Leo smiled. His whole face lit up. His hands thumped on Alessandro's arm and he crowed with delight.

Terrific! Her son had developed a soft spot for a man who never wanted to see him.

Obstinately Carys shied from dwelling on the sight of her son in his father's arms. It would be the only time. It was foolish to feel even a jot of sentimentality over the image of the tall, strong man holding her precious baby so ineptly yet so securely.

Carys hurried forward, arms outstretched.

'I'll take him.'

Alessandro didn't even turn his head. He was busy regarding Leo, not even flinching when the child's rhythmic thumps against his arm became real whacks as he grew impatient with the adult's lack of response.

'Alessandro?' Her voice was husky. The intensity of his stare as he looked down at his son made something flip over in her stomach. Anxiety walked its fingers down her spine.

'I'll arrange for the necessary tests to be done as soon as possible. Someone will ring you tomorrow with the details.'

'Tests?'

He didn't even turn at the sound of her voice, but he did lift Leo a little closer, winning himself a gurgle of approval and a spate of excited Leo-speak.

Carys watched Leo lean up, patting both hands over Alessandro's square, scrupulously shaved jaw. A squiggle of emotion unsettled her, seeing her little boy with the man she'd once loved.

If only circumstances had been different.

No! It was better she knew what sort of man Alessandro was and that in his eyes she could never measure up.

'DNA tests, of course.' He flashed an assessing look from slitted eyes. 'You can't expect me to take your word this is my son.'

Her stomach went into freefall.

She'd fought so hard to have Alessandro acknowledge his son before giving up in despair. Yet now she felt fear at his sudden interest. Fear at what this might mean.

Leo was hers. But if Alessandro decided he wanted him...

She found refuge in stormy anger. 'Distrust must be your middle name, Alessandro.'

The idea of him seeking independent scientific proof was a slap in the face.

Especially as he'd been her only lover.

His distrust tainted what they'd shared, reducing it to something tawdry. Her skin crawled as she met his glittering gaze and felt the weight of his doubt.

His fiery green stare scorched her. 'Better distrustful than gullible.'

CHAPTER SEVEN

THREE days later Carys received a summons to the presidential suite. David, her manager, relayed the news with a quizzical look that made the blood rise hot in her cheeks.

'Moving in exalted circles, Carys,' he murmured. 'Don't hurry back.'

She was aware of the other staff, watching surreptitiously as she pushed her chair back and stood up.

Carys had been a bundle of nerves for the past few days, ever since Alessandro had pulled strings to have the DNA tests taken in the privacy of her flat. Another reminder, if she'd needed it, of his enormous wealth. His ability to get what he wanted.

The technician had been friendly, talkative despite the marked silence between Carys and Alessandro. She'd seemed oblivious to the atmosphere laden with unspoken challenges and questions. Or maybe the woman was used to the high-octane emotions such circumstances engendered. After all, there'd be no need for mouth swabs and scientific proof if there was trust between a couple.

If a man believed his lover.

Sucking in her breath, Carys straightened her shoulders and took her time walking to the lift.

Alessandro must have received advice from the pathology company. Surely that was why she'd been summoned. No doubt he'd paid for the privilege of getting an ultra-fast turnaround on the lab results.

Her stomach cramped in anxiety.

What would he do now that he knew Leo was his?

The question had haunted her for days so that even when she finally slept, stress dreams plagued her. She woke feeling even more tired than when she went to bed.

The butler was waiting at the door for her, his smile friendly but impersonal.

Had he seen her desperate flight from the suite several days ago? Carys kept her chin high as she forced an answering smile to her lips and walked in.

The lush quiet of the suite engulfed her. Its understated opulence showcased fine furnishings and every modern convenience provided just for one man. It had been designed for the mega-wealthy, the vastly important.

No wonder she felt wretchedly small and nervous as she approached the silent man who dominated the room.

He might fit in here, but she didn't. Carys was completely, unalterably ordinary. Not by any stretch of the imagination could she be considered special. She'd faced that long ago, before Alessandro had tempted her for a brief, crazy time to believe in miracles.

'Carys.' The sound of his deep, slightly husky voice rippled like a sensual caress across her skin. Her reaction, her physical weakness for him, made her hackles rise.

'Alessandro.' She nodded. 'You demanded my presence?'

His head tilted slightly as he watched her, his look assessing but his face unreadable.

'I *requested* your presence.'

'Ah, but when the request comes from the presidential suite we staff tend to jump.' For some reason she found safety in emphasising the huge gulf between them. As if she could magically erase the memory of the madness that had gripped them last time she was here.

Her gaze flickered to the plump lounges, the wall where he'd held her and caressed her and almost...

'Please, take a seat.'

To her surprise, he gestured to an upright chair in front of an antique desk. Carys shot him a startled glance but complied. Better this than the intimacy of the sofas.

It was only as she sat that she noticed the papers spread across the desk. 'You've had the test results, then.'

'I have.'

Carys could read nothing in his voice or in his face. Was he disappointed, angry, excited to discover he had a son? Or, she thought with a sinking sensation, didn't he feel anything at all?

'Coffee, Robson. Or—' Alessandro paused to catch her eye '—would you prefer tea?'

'Nothing, thank you.' The idea of swallowing anything made her stomach curdle.

'That will be all, Robson.' Alessandro waited till the butler left before he turned to her again.

Instead of taking a chair, he lounged, arms crossed, against the desk. He was near enough for her to register his cologne. Her nerves reacted with a shimmy of excitement that made her grit her teeth in annoyance. She wished he'd move away. Far enough that she wasn't plagued by remnants of the physical attraction that had been so strong between them.

'What is it you want, Alessandro?' After days of silence from him, now he expected her jump to do his bidding. It infuriated her.

'We have arrangements to make. And you need to sign this.' He waved a hand towards the paper on the desk then reached into his jacket pocket, eyes still holding hers. 'You can use this when you've read it.'

Casually he laid a gold fountain pen on the desk beside a wad of papers.

Carys turned to face the desk. Not lab results after all. A quick look showed her long numbered paragraphs. Dense typescript. Pages and pages of legalese.

Her heart sank. Just the sort of document she hated. She couldn't deal with this while Alessandro stood so close.

A flutter of panic flared in her breast and she reached out one clammy hand to flick through the wad. The last page had space for her signature and Alessandro's.

As the pages settled again, she tried to concentrate on the

first paragraph, but one of the lines kept jumping sideways so she lost her place.

Damn. Had she brought her glasses? She fumbled in her jacket pocket, aware of Alessandro's silent scrutiny.

'What is it you want me to sign?'

His eyes blazed green fire as he watched her from his superior height. Did she imagine a hint of tension around his mouth? A faint tightness between his brows?

'A prenuptial agreement.'

'*A what?*' Carys' reading glasses slid from numb fingers as she swung round to face him.

The sober light in his eyes told her she wasn't hearing things.

'An agreement setting out both parties' entitlements—'

'I know what a prenuptial agreement is.' She dragged in a deep breath to fill her suddenly constricted lungs, her pulse racing jaggedly. 'We don't need one. It's for people who plan to marry.'

He smiled then. Not a grin. Not even a real smile. Just a brief quirk of the lips that might have signalled amusement or impatience or even annoyance.

And still his eyes bored into her like lasers.

'We need it, Carys.' His words were crisp, clear and unmistakeable. 'Because we're getting married.'

He reached out and stroked a finger down her cheek. Fire streaked across her skin and blasted through her hard won calm. 'It's the only possible course of action. You must have known we'd marry once I discovered the child is mine.'

For an eternity the words hung between them. She stared up at him, lush mouth sagging, bright eyes stunned. Then, like the flick of a switch, animation returned.

'*The child* has a name, damn you!'

Carys jerked from his touch, catapulting from the chair and almost knocking it over in her haste. She stood defiant and furious, feet planted squarely and chest heaving.

'Don't you *ever* talk about Leo again as if he were some… some commodity!'

Madonna mia! With her eyes flashing and high colour in her softly-rounded cheeks, energy radiating from her in angry waves, she was stunning. More than pretty. Or beautiful. Something far more profound.

Enough almost to distract him from the important business of securing his child.

Alessandro felt the drag of attraction in his belly, his limbs, his mind. It was the possessive hunger he'd felt for days but mixed with another sensation so deep-seated it rocked him where he stood.

In that moment the careful logic that dictated his decision to marry faded. This was no longer about simple logic. The force that drove him was purely visceral.

She would be his. He would accept no other alternative.

He would have Carys *and* his son. A wave of hot pleasure suffused him.

'Of course he's not a commodity. He's Leonardo.' Alessandro inclined his head, savouring the name. 'Leo Mattani.'

An image of intelligent jade eyes, handsome dark hair and a small determined chin surfaced. His son.

His son!

Satisfaction and pride welled in his chest and—

'No! Leo Wells, not Leo Mattani. And that won't change. Marriage is a preposterous idea, so you can forget it.' Carys took a step closer, her chin rising.

Once more a blast of white-hot hunger shot through him.

What a woman she was! So fiercely protective and proud.

And as a lover…? Alessandro inhaled sharply, breathing in her skin's warm cinnamon scent. He looked forward to rediscovering the passion they'd shared. It must have been spectacular for him to take the unprecedented step of inviting her to live with him.

But first, most important, he would secure his son.

A twist of deep-seated memory skewered Alessandro, ripping a familiar hole through his belly. Of the feckless way his own mother had abandoned her '*caro Sandro*' without a backward glance. How selfish greed had triumphed over the supposedly unbreakable bonds of maternal love. She'd put her own salacious desires and hunger for wealth above her son.

Despite Carys' fiery attitude and her protectiveness, Alessandro knew the frailty of maternal love. The fickleness of women.

He would safeguard his son. Shield him and ensure he never wanted for anything.

The terms of the prenuptial agreement, with its hefty allowance for Carys while she stayed with him and his son, would ensure stability in Leo's life.

Alessandro's legal team had worked night and day to make it watertight. The obscene amount of money Alessandro had allocated to buy his wife would keep her just where he wanted her. Where Leo needed her.

With Alessandro.

'My son will grow up as Leo Mattani. That is not open to debate.' Alessandro waved his hand dismissively, his expression remote. 'Any other alternative is unthinkable.'

'Unthinkable?' Carys planted her hands on her hips as she stared into the proud, arrogant face of the man she'd once loved. 'He's been Leo Wells since he was born and he's been just fine, thank you very much.'

'Just fine?' Alessandro shook his head abruptly, voice deepening and nostrils flaring with disapproval, the epitome of masculine scorn. 'You think it fine that my son is born illegitimate?'

For a moment Carys stared helplessly into his dark, heated gaze, reading indignation and outrage.

In a perfect world Leo would have been born into a loving family with parents who were permanently committed to each other. But that hadn't been an option.

'There are worse things in the world,' she said quietly, wrapping her arms round her torso as old pain tore through her. The pain of lacerated dreams.

She'd done everything she could to ensure Alessandro had known about her pregnancy. But even if he'd known, even if he'd proposed marriage, nothing could change the fact that he wasn't a man she could trust with her heart. Or that she'd never fit into his world.

Silence hung between them as he stared down at her.

'And you think my son will continue to be *just fine* growing up in a run-down tenement among thieves and pimps?' One haughty eyebrow rose to a lofty height and Carys felt the weight of his disapproval push down on her.

'You're exaggerating,' she countered, ignoring a twinge of guilt that she hadn't been able to find somewhere better. 'It's not that bad. Besides, I'm planning to move.'

'Really? And how will you find better premises on your wage?'

His supercilious tone made Carys bite her lip in frustration. It didn't matter that her salary was the best she could get with her qualifications or that she worked hard for the money she earned. In the long term her prospects were good for promotion. But in the meantime…

'I will provide for Leo. I always have.'

For a moment Alessandro's gaze seemed to soften. 'It must have been difficult, managing on your own.'

Carys shrugged. She didn't dwell on that. On the fact that her siblings and father, scattered as they were around the globe, hadn't found time to visit when Leo was born, or afterwards. They'd sent gifts instead. A money box from her advertising executive sister in Perth. A set of children's books Leo couldn't read for years from her physicist brother in New Zealand. An oversized fluffy rabbit from her brother at a medical outpost in New Guinea. And from her dad in Canada money to secure the bond on her flat.

They meant well and they cared in their distant, uninvolved way. But how she'd longed for one of them to make the effort to be with her when she'd felt so alone. When depression had vied with excitement and determination as she struggled on her own.

Defiantly Carys met the eyes of the one person who'd had the right to be at her side when Leo came into the world.

But that time was past.

'I'm used to managing alone.' Years younger than her siblings, the late child of parents engrossed in demanding careers, she'd virtually brought herself up. 'Leo and I are OK.'

'OK isn't enough for my son. He deserves more.'

Carys compressed her lips, fighting the urge to agree. The

doting mother in her wanted Leo to have the best opportunities. The sort of opportunities a working single mum couldn't provide.

'What Leo needs is love and a secure, nurturing environment. I give him that.' She defied him to disagree.

'Of course he does. And we'll provide it. Together.'

Had Alessandro stepped closer? His eyes mesmerised and his persuasive dark coffee tone made the impossible sound almost sensible.

Carys gave herself a mental shake.

'There's no question of *together.* What we had is over.'

It died two years ago, when you betrayed me with another woman then accused me of being unfaithful. She didn't say it out loud. There was no point in revisiting the past. Carys had to focus on the future, on what was best for Leo.

'It will never be over, Carys.' His voice dropped to a caress, like the stroke of velvet on bare, shivery skin. 'We have a child together.'

She clasped her hands before her, horrified to find them shaking. His words conjured images that were too vivid, too enticing, of what it had been like when they'd been lovers.

'But that's no reason for marriage! You'll have access to him, see him as he grows.' It was a father's right. Besides, despite the emotional turmoil it would cause her to see Alessandro regularly, it was a relief that Leo would grow up knowing his father. Every boy deserved—

'Access?' The word shot out like bullet. 'You think that's what I want? What my son needs?'

This time it wasn't her imagination. Alessandro obliterated the space between them with a single stride. He loomed above her like an impregnable mountain citadel. Unmoving and unforgiving. Utterly forbidding.

She trembled at the impact of his powerful presence. Energy radiated from him. A dangerous undercurrent of power.

'You have strange ideas about fatherhood. I've already missed the first year of my son's life. I don't intend to miss any more.' His clipped words revealed gleaming white teeth as they bit out each word. Involuntarily Carys shrank a little.

'I just meant—'

'I know what you meant.' He paused, scrutinising her as if she came from another planet. 'Leo is my son. My flesh, my blood. I refuse to be a part-time visitor in his life while he grows up on the other side of the world.'

'But marriage!' Her tongue stuck to the roof of her mouth on the word. 'The idea is absurd.'

Alessandro's eyes darkened. His face stiffened and his lips thinned. 'I assumed you'd prefer that to the alternative.'

'Alternative?' Carys' voice was a cracked whisper as foreboding slammed into her. That look in his eyes...

'A legal battle for custody.'

CHAPTER EIGHT

CARYS' fingers twisted into knots as he said the words she'd been dreading. She swallowed convulsively, forcing down fear. 'I'm his mother. Any court would give me custody.'

'You're sure, Carys?' An infinitesimal shake of his dark head accompanied the words, as if he pitied her naivety. 'You have a good lawyer? As good as my legal team?'

Plus the Mattani millions to back them up. The words were unspoken, but Carys heard them nonetheless.

'You wouldn't…' Her voice petered out as she met his unblinking stare. He would. He'd do what it took to get Leo.

Jerkily she swung away, frantic for breathing space. For time to marshal her jumbled thoughts. Her chest cramped so she could barely breathe and her head pounded as tension crawled up her spine and wrapped clammy fingers around her temples.

He was wrong. He must be! No court would take a child from his mother.

And yet…Carys stumbled to a stop in front of a massive window commanding a view of the city. Alessandro's wealth and power were far beyond anything she or her family, if they were so inclined, could gather. He lived in a world of stratospherically rich, privileged and well-connected families. The normal rules didn't apply to them.

Did she dare take Alessandro on? She should have nothing to worry about. She was a good mother. Leo was thriving.

Yet the poisonous seed of doubt grew.

The thought of their cramped flat in a run-down neighbourhood, the best she could provide on her meagre wage, haunted her. Would that be held against her? Contrasted to the vast resources of the Mattani family?

There were so many ways Alessandro could get what he wanted, even without gaining sole custody. What if he refused to return Leo after a visit? If he kept him in Italy?

Carys didn't have the resources to go there and demand her son back. She didn't have the power to force Alessandro's hand. She'd be at his mercy. Who knew what delays Alessandro could throw up to stop her seeing Leo while their lawyers slogged it out?

A shiver rippled through her and she lifted a hand to her throbbing temple. This was the stuff of nightmares.

The man she'd loved wouldn't have threatened her like this, no matter how they'd parted. He'd never have robbed her of her baby.

But that man was gone. The realisation felt like someone had carved a part out of her heart. Alessandro had no memory of the happiness they'd once shared. To him she was merely a stranger who had what he wanted.

She longed to hold Leo, safe and warm in her arms. Hide away from Alessandro and his demands.

But there was no hiding.

'My preference is to keep this between us, Carys.' His deep voice came from just behind her, making her jump. 'I wouldn't *choose* a court battle. That would be a last resort.'

He expected her to be grateful for that? Hurt and fear coalesced in a surge of desperate anger till her body hummed with the effort of containing it.

'Well, that's a comfort! I feel so much better now.'

Long fingers grasped her shoulder, their heat branding through her clothes. She resisted but his grip firmed and she turned.

Was that compassion in his gaze?

She blinked and the illusion disappeared. Alessandro's face was angular, hard, powerful. He would never back down.

'You come swanning into our lives and think you can run roughshod over everyone.' Her words tumbled out so fast they slurred. 'As if only you know best.' Carys drew herself up to her full height. 'Your demands are outrageous. You've got no right—'

'I have the right of a father.' His cool words stopped her tirade. 'Remember that, Carys. You are no longer the only one with a say in how our son is brought up.'

Our son. The words were a douche of cold water dousing her indignation. Reminding her how vulnerable she was.

'I offer you marriage, Carys. Position, wealth, a life of ease. And—' he paused '—a home for our son. He will grow up with both parents. In a secure, stable home. What objection can you have to that?'

'But we don't care for each other. How can we—?'

'We have the best possible reason to marry. To bring up our child. That's something worthwhile and enduring.' The words sank into the silence between them as his touch warmed her shoulder. She wanted to pull away, but his intense gaze pinioned her. 'There is no better reason to wed.'

Except love. The futile little voice rang in her ears.

Carys ignored it. She'd given up believing in seductive fantasies of romance two years ago.

Yet she couldn't douse her dismay at the matter-of-fact way Alessandro spoke of marriage for the sake of their child. Perhaps the aristocracy were accustomed to convenient marriages, brokered for family or business reasons.

How could she marry a man she didn't love? A man who'd betrayed her trust?

Her lips twisted ruefully. Look where her fantasies of love had got her!

'Unless…' His fingers tightened then dropped away. His head jerked up and he regarded her down the length of his aristocratic nose, his look coldly accusing. 'Unless you've become attached to someone here?'

Carys hesitated, tempted to grab at the excuse. But she couldn't lie. Once already she'd tried to deflect Alessandro's interest by pretending to have a boyfriend, but she hadn't been able to maintain the pretence.

She shook her head, shifting back a pace and turning her head away. He was too close for comfort.

Did he know how distracting he was, standing in her personal space, radiating energy like a human generator? The hairs on her arms prickled just being so near him.

'Good, then there's no reason to refuse.'

'But what if…?' Carys bit her tongue, furious that she'd begun to blurt out her wayward thoughts. Furious she was even listening to his bizarre reasoning. She must be mad.

'What if…?' His whisper made her shiver and stiffen as the warmth of his breath caressed her cheek.

For three heartbeats, for four, Carys remained silent. Then unwillingly she continued. 'What if one day you meet someone you…care for? Someone you want to marry?'

Even now, cured of the love she'd felt for Alessandro, the thought of him with someone else squeezed her insides into a tortured knot of distress.

'That won't happen.' Certainty throbbed in his words and she turned, curiosity stirring at his instantaneous response.

'You can't know that.'

Alessandro's beautiful, sensuous mouth kicked up at the corner in a mirthless smile that made a mockery of the heat she'd imagined in his eyes moments before.

'I know it absolutely.' His gaze held hers till her chest tightened and she remembered to breathe. And still his expression of weary cynicism didn't change. 'Romantic love is a fallacy invented for the gullible. Only a fool would consider himself in love, much less marry for it.'

Carys felt her eyes widen, staring up at the man she'd once believed she'd known. He'd been considerate, witty, urbane and, above all, passionate. The sort of lover a woman dreamed about. A lover who tempted a woman to believe in the most outrageously wonderful happily ever afters.

She'd always understood he kept something of himself back. She'd sensed his deep-seated reserve despite the intimacies they shared. A sense of aloneness she'd never quite breached. An aloneness that intensified after his father died and Alessandro withdrew, devoting himself to business. Yet it shocked her to discover the hardened kernel of scepticism behind his charming exterior.

It made him seem so *empty*.

Had he always been like that? Or was this the result of the trauma he'd been through?

Distress and unwilling compassion burgeoned for this man who seemed to have so much, yet apparently felt so little.

Absurdly she wanted to reach out to him.

And what? Comfort him? Show him compassion? Love?

No! She reeled back, stunned at the depth of feelings he engendered even now.

Her hand, half raised as if to reach out to him, dropped noiselessly to her side.

'Marriage is a duty,' he continued, oblivious to her reaction. 'There was never any question of me marrying for love.' His scornful tone almost made her wince, recalling how blithely she'd believed he was falling in love with her as she'd fallen for him.

Acidly she wondered how he'd class his interest in other women. Even if he were married, there would be other women. Alessandro was a man who enjoyed sex. He wouldn't stay celibate just because he'd married a woman he didn't love. He'd have no qualms about pursuing someone who took his fancy. After all, she'd been his bit on the side, hadn't she?

'I believe in marriage for life.' His words cut through her stark thoughts. 'Once married there would be no divorce.'

'A life sentence, in fact.'

'You would not find it so hard, believe me, Carys.' A hint of mellow honey edged his words and Carys shut her eyes, fighting the insidious weakness in her bones. He was talking about money, luxury, position, that was all. Not anything important, like the emotions he so despised.

'You're not worried I might fall for someone else and want a divorce?' The words tumbled out in self-defence.

Taut silence reigned as his displeasure vibrated on the air between them.

'There will be no divorce.' His words were adamant, his tone rough-edged. 'As for believing yourself in love…'

Abruptly he stepped in front of her and lifted her chin with his hand. She felt herself fall into the shaded depths of his green gaze. Heat sparked in her abdomen as he leaned closer. A thrill of excitement skimmed down her backbone.

No! She wasn't making a fool of herself like that again. If he thought he could seduce her into falling for him all over again, he had another thing coming.

Furiously she jerked out of his hold. 'Don't worry,' her voice was icy with disdain. 'There's no danger of me falling in love with *anyone*.'

Once bitten, now cured for life!

His eyes blazed with curiosity. Then those heavy lids dropped, hiding his expression.

'Good. Then we have an understanding.'

'Now, just a minute! I didn't say I—'

'I'll leave you to read the agreement.' He gestured to the papers on the desk as he turned away, obviously eager to go. 'There are arrangements to be made.' He paused, spearing her with a look. 'Consider well what I've said, Carys. I'll be back soon for your answer.'

She hadn't meant to, but finally Carys was drawn to the elegant regency desk with its fateful document. The thickly worded pages taunted her, evidence of Alessandro's superior position, of his lawyers and his precious money.

She wasn't really considering marriage. Was she? Fear swooped through her stomach and her damp hands clenched.

Alessandro couldn't force her to marry.

He was gambling that a judge would give him custody. More, he was probably bluffing about court action. He wouldn't…

The memory of eyes flashing like jade daggers in the sun pulled her up short.

He would. To get his son, of course he would.

How had she ever imagined Alessandro would settle for part-time fatherhood?

Stiffly she raised a hand and drew the papers towards her. She settled her glasses on her nose and began reading.

By the third page panic welled. It had taken twenty minutes of desperate concentration and still some of the text eluded her.

She was exhausted after so many sleepless nights and emotionally drained. Even at the best of times her dyslexia made reading solid text like this a challenge. But now…she bit her lip, fighting down angry tears of frustration.

Leo's future was at stake and she didn't have the skills to ensure he was protected! What sort of mother was she?

The old, jeering voice in her head told her she was a failure, and for a moment she was tempted to believe it.

She slammed her palms on the table and pushed her chair away. It wasn't a matter of skills or intelligence. It was simply a disability, exacerbated by tiredness and stress.

Besides—it suddenly hit her—the prenup wasn't about Leo. It was about her rights and Alessandro's.

She flicked to the end and found a section, mercifully short, that declared she would get nothing, either in cash or interest in Alessandro's fortune, in the case of divorce. Relief filled her. That was the heart of it. All the rest was legal bumph of conditions and counter-conditions.

Still, caution warned she should have a lawyer read this before she signed.

Hell! Caution warned her to run a mile rather than consider marrying Alessandro Mattani! Even in a convenient marriage where they'd be virtual strangers, he had the power to turn her world on its head.

But this wasn't about her. This was about Leo. Leo who had the right to both his parents. Who didn't deserve to be fought over in a tug-of-love battle. Whom she loved so much she couldn't bear the risk of Alessandro taking him from her.

Carys blinked glazing hot eyes and straightened her spine.

She didn't have a lawyer to check the document, but that didn't matter. She didn't have a choice.

Heart heavy, fingers tense, she picked up Alessandro's custom-made pen and turned to the final page.

Carys Antoinette Wells. Such a pompous document deserved her full name. But instead of writing with a flourish, her hand shook so much it looked like the signature of an inexperienced teenager, pretending to be someone else.

The pen clattered to the desk. Carys got slowly to her feet, stiff like an old woman, her heart leaden.

A muffled sound drew Alessandro's attention. He lifted his head, all too ready for a distraction from paperwork.

These last days Alessandro had found it extraordinarily difficult to give business his full attention. To be expected since he'd just discovered he had a son and was in the process of acquiring a wife.

A renegade spurt of pleasure shot through him. At the thought of Leo. And, more surprisingly, at the idea of Carys, soon to be his wife.

His lips twisted in self-mockery. Two years of celibacy had honed his libido to a razor-sharp edge. That explained the anticipation surging in his blood. Even the freshly recovered memory, visited again and again, of her lying in his bed, dark russet hair spread in sensual abandon, seized his muscles in potent sexual excitement.

Since the accident his sex drive had been dormant. At first he hadn't given it a thought. All his physical and mental strength had been directed to recovery. Then there were the gruelling hours he'd put in day after day, month after month, to turn around the family company that had careened towards disaster.

Yet as the months passed, he'd realised something fundamental had altered. Despite the temptations around him, he barely found the energy to take out a pretty girl, much less summon the enthusiasm to have one in his bed.

He'd always been a discriminating but active lover. Twenty-two months of celibacy was unheard of.

Was it any wonder he fretted over those lost months, as if something in that time had reduced his drive? Somehow weakened his very masculinity?

Not even to himself had he admitted anxiety that the change in him might be permanent.

Now though, there was no doubt everything was in working order. There was a permanent ache in his groin as he fought to stifle the lustful desires Carys provoked.

His lips stretched taut in a smile of hungry anticipation.

The sound came again. A whimper, drawing Alessandro's attention. He turned to find Leo stirring in his mother's arms. She'd refused to let the cabin crew take the boy but had stretched out on her bed with the tot in her arms. They'd looked so comfortable together Alessandro saw no reason to object.

Now the little one was fidgeting and twisting in his mother's loose embrace.

Alessandro watched his son's vigorous movements and felt again the cataclysmic surge of wonder that had overcome him when he'd held the boy in his arms. The idea that he had a child still stunned him.

Green eyes caught green and Leo stopped his restless jigging.

'Ba,' Leo said solemnly. 'Ba, ba, ba.'

Alessandro put his laptop aside. 'No. It's papa.'

'Baba!' One small arm stretched towards him and pride flared. His son was intelligent, that was obvious.

Alessandro stood, scooped the boy off the bed and held him carefully in both arms. An only child himself, Alessandro had virtually no experience with young children. But he'd learn fast, for his son's sake.

He'd been brought up by nannies and tutors, following a strict regimen designed to ensure he grew early into self-reliance and emotional independence. Alessandro didn't intend to spoil his son, but he'd ensure Leo spent time with his father—a luxury Alessandro had rarely enjoyed.

He lifted his son higher, registering the elusive scent he'd noticed before, of baby, sunshine and talc. He inhaled deeply and found himself staring into a small bright face.

'I'm Papa,' he murmured, brushing dark hair back from his son's forehead. It was silky and warm under his palm.

'Baba!' Leo's grin was infectious and Alessandro's lips tilted in an answering curve.

'Come. It's time to get better acquainted.' He turned towards his seat but paused as he caught sight of Carys. She lay on her side, arms outstretched invitingly.

In sleep she looked serene, gentle, tempting.

What was it about her that tempted him when so many

beauties hadn't? That turned him on so that just standing looking down at her, he was hard as granite with wanting. Desire was a slow unmistakeable throb in his blood.

She was the mother of his child, and that was a definite turn on. The thought of her body swelling and ripening with his baby was intensely erotic and satisfying.

But he'd lusted after her before he knew about Leo. When she was a stranger in a photograph.

Why was she different?

Because she challenged him and provoked him and got under his skin till he wanted to kiss her into submission?

Or because of something they'd shared?

Something about Carys Wells made him hanker to believe she was different.

Different! Ha!

She'd admitted she had left him because he'd found out about her with another man. Stefano Manzoni. The very shark who'd been circling, aiming to take a fatal bite out of Alessandro's company after Leonardo Mattani's death. That added insult to injury.

The idea of Carys with Stefano made Alessandro sick to the stomach. Had the affair been consummated? Fury pounded through him at the images his mind conjured.

He'd make absolutely sure from now on that Carys had no time to think of looking at another man.

Then there was the way she'd pored over the prenup in Melbourne. Proof, if he'd needed any, that she was just like the rest. She'd been so absorbed, she hadn't heard him enter then leave again.

Of course she'd signed without any further demur. As soon as she'd read the size of the outrageously large allowance he'd grant her while she lived with him and Leo, she'd been hooked. Just as he'd intended.

The generosity of that allowance had caused a stir with his advisers, but Alessandro knew what he was doing. He'd make sure Leo had the stability of a mother who stayed. Alessandro's son wouldn't be left, abandoned, as he had been.

No. Despite her strange allure, Carys wasn't different.

And yet…there would be compensations.

He looked from her abandoned sprawl and enticingly sensual lips to the chubby face of the son in his arms.

He'd made the right decision.

Carys didn't know whether to be relieved or astonished that Alessandro didn't take them to his home in the hills above Lake Como. She'd loved the spare elegance of his modern architect-designed house, built to catch every view with spectacular windows and an innovative design.

Now though, he drove his snarling, low-slung car to the massive family villa. *The villa to which she'd never been invited during her months living with him.*

She hadn't been good enough for his family.

The knowledge stuck like a jagged block of ice in her chest as he turned into a wide gravel drive. Her breathing slowed as trepidation filled her.

They passed lawns and garden beds, artfully planted shrubberies, and emerged before a spectacular view of the lake. To the left the villa rose serenely, like a sugar-encrusted period fantasy. To the right stretched Lake Como: indigo water rimmed by small towns and sunlit slopes.

Beside her sat Alessandro in silent magnificence. Six feet two of brooding Italian male. His straight brows and thinned lips made it clear how he felt about bringing her to the family mansion. Clearly she wasn't the sort of bride he'd have chosen in other circumstances.

The knowledge ate at her like acid. She hadn't been good enough before. Now only Leo's presence in the back seat elevated her enough to enter the Mattani inner sanctum.

Carys sensed old doubts circling, the belief that she really was second best, not able to live up to her family's exacting standards, let alone Alessandro's.

The sight of the villa, redolent with generations of power and wealth, only reinforced the sinking sense of inadequacy she'd striven all her life to overcome.

'Your home is very imposing,' she murmured as she shoved the traitorous thoughts away. She would *not* go down th t track. Only tiredness made her think that way.

Plus nerves about what lay ahead.

'You think so?' Alessandro shrugged. 'I've always thought it overdone, as if trying too hard to impress.' He waved towards one end of the villa, thickly encrusted with pillars, balconies, decorative arched windows and even what looked from this angle like a turret.

'I hadn't thought about it like that.' She scanned the pale silvery-pink façade, taking in every quaint architectural device, every ostentatious finish. Alessandro was right. Yet with its mellow stone bathed in morning sun it was beautiful. 'Now you mention it, it's rather like an ageing showgirl, a little overdone, a little too obvious. But appealing anyway.'

A shout of laughter made her turn. Alessandro leaned back in his seat. He grinned as he met her startled gaze. That grin brought back crazy, wonderful memories. Her heart jumped then began pounding against her ribcage as heat sizzled, a long slow burn, right to her heart.

'You've hit the nail on the head. I'd never have described it that way, but you're absolutely right.' His gaze met hers and a shock wave hit her at the glint of approval and pleasure in his eyes. 'Just don't let Livia hear you say that. It's her pride and joy.'

'Livia?' The surge of jubilation Carys had felt in the unexpected shared moment ebbed. 'Is your stepmother here?'

'She no longer lives here. She spends her time in Milan or Rome. But you'll see her. She'll give you advice on what's expected of you. Fill you in on the social background you need to know.'

And you can't? The thought remained unspoken.

Of course he couldn't. Alessandro would be too busy with business or with other interests to spare time for his new fiancée. Swiftly Carys thrust aside the idea of his 'other interests' and schooled her face into a calm façade.

'Is that necessary?' She met his steady look then turned away to fumble with her seat belt. 'I'm sure she's busy.'

And she never liked me anyway.

Spending time teaching the ropes to a gauche plebeian whose sense of style began and ended with chain-store bargains would be hell for Livia. And worse for Carys.

'Not too busy to assist my bride.' His cool tone reinforced what Carys already knew, that this would be a duty for the older woman, not a pleasure.

'I'll look forward to it,' Carys said through gritted teeth and turned away, only to find her door already open. A man in a butler's uniform bowed, waiting for her to step out.

'*Grazie*,' she murmured, dredging up her rusty Italian.

He smiled and bowed deeper. 'Welcome, madam. It's a pleasure to have you here.'

Delight warmed her as she realised she could understand his clear, precise Italian. It had been almost two years since she'd spoken it, but she had an ear for languages. Perhaps because she'd spent so many years honing her memory and learning by heart at school. She'd discovered that was the best way to avoid revising with reams of written notes.

Hesitantly she tried out a little more Italian as she got out of the car. She was gratified when Paulo, the butler, encouraged her faltering attempts. Soon he was telling her about the comforts of the villa awaiting her, including a lavish morning tea, and she was responding.

Carys let him usher her from the car, only to pull up short at the sight of Alessandro waiting for her.

He held Leo, still slumbering, in his arms. For a moment the sight of her son, flushed with sleep and hair tousled, snuggled up against the wide shoulder of his magnificent, handsome father, made her heart falter in its rhythm.

Then Alessandro spoke, fortunately in a voice pitched only for her ears. 'If you've finished practising your charm on my staff we can go in.'

Confused, Carys met his searing dark scrutiny.

'Now we're marrying, you need to forget about winning other men's smiles.' His grim tone made it clear he wasn't joking. 'My wife needs to be above reproach.'

'You think I was *flirting?*' Amazement coloured her voice.

She could scarcely credit it. Alessandro sounded almost…
jealous.

The idea was preposterous. But the glitter of disapproval in
his eyes intrigued her.

She imagined things. Alessandro had wanted her sexually in
Melbourne only because she was convenient and shamingly
willing. But that was past. Now he saw her solely as Leo's
mother. He hadn't touched her since he'd discovered his son.
Clearly he wanted her for Leo not himself.

Carys thanked her lucky stars for that. It gave her distance.
Safety. For if he ever decided to seduce her again, she wasn't sure
she had the strength to resist.

'I think it's time we went in and settled our son,' he said,
ignoring her blurted question. He breached the distance between
them, consuming her personal space till she found it almost impossible to draw a steady breath. 'You'll be tired after the journey
and you need rest before this afternoon.'

'This afternoon?' Bemused, Carys shook her head.

'Livia has arranged a designer to fit you for your wedding dress.'
His lips curved up in a tight smile that could have signalled either
pleasure or stoic acceptance. 'We marry at the end of the week.'

CHAPTER NINE

FOUR hours later Carys waited, palms damp with trepidation, for the haute couture designer who'd been brought in to produce her wedding gown.

The fact that Alessandro's name could procure a top designer to dress her in such a short time only reinforced his enormous wealth and the huge gulf between them. Carys had never had anything made to order in her life.

The few high-fashion gurus she'd met while working had been condescending creatures. Perhaps because they took one look at her: average height, average face, unfashionably rounded figure, and knew she was no clothes horse.

At least this one already knew the worst. Alessandro had insisted on having her measurements taken in Melbourne and sent through to Milan, with a rather unflattering photo.

Carys glanced at her watch. Maybe the designer wouldn't show. Maybe they'd decided the challenge of passing her off as anything approaching chic was too hard.

She grimaced as she paced the salon, wishing the appointment was somewhere less imposing. The luxurious formality of the reception rooms stifled. Carefully she avoided the gilt-edged antique mirrors and stiff, silk-upholstered chairs. She felt like an ugly duckling, plucked out of her comfortable little pond and plonked in a palace.

If only she'd been allowed to buy a ready-made dress.

Despite her nerves, her lips twitched as she remembered

Alessandro's look of astonishment when she suggested it. Only a big formal wedding would do for the Conte Mattani and his bride. No quick civil ceremony was permitted.

So now she had to face a temperamental artiste, no doubt disappointed the bride wouldn't live up to their designs. Carys stood straighter, preparing for the worst.

A knock sounded on the massive double doors and Paulo's voice introduced her visitor. Carys felt her jaw lock as his words rolled over her. Her body stiffened with disbelief.

Impossible as it seemed, the worst was even more horrendous than she could have anticipated.

Her stomach went into a freefall of shock.

How could Livia have done it? How could she have chosen this designer of all people? She must have known—

'Signorina Wells?' The softly spoken words finally penetrated. Reluctantly, stiffly, Carys turned.

The woman before her was just as she remembered. Slim, elegant, huge dark eyes in a gorgeous elfin face. Dressed with a casual grace and a fortune in pearls that accentuated her delicate appeal.

Was it any wonder Alessandro had planned to marry her?

Pain, razor sharp and vicious, sheared through Carys. She grabbed the back of a nearby chair rather than double up in anguish. Desperate tension crawled up her spine as she strove to school her expression.

'Principessa Carlotta.' The words were rusty, thick, the product of a throat aching with distress.

Did they really expect her to submit to this woman's ministrations?

'Carlotta, please.' Her smile was warm, her husky voice appealing. Carys registered surprise that she seemed so approachable. So apparently ready to befriend the woman Alessandro had chosen over her.

Carys knew if their places were reversed she couldn't behave so blithely.

'Forgive me.' The other woman stopped a few paces away, her

smile disappearing as concern etched her brow. 'But are you all right? You look very pale.'

Carys wasn't surprised. It felt as if all her blood had drained away. She clamped her hand tighter around the chair back, summoning the strength she needed to stay upright.

'I'm…' What? Surprised to find my husband's ex-lover here? *Or was she still his lover?*

The thought smashed through her rigid self-control and Carys found her knees crumpling. Abruptly she sat, grateful to discover an antique sofa behind her.

'You're unwell. I'll call for assistance.'

'No!' Carys cringed at the idea of a fuss. She couldn't believe her own weakness. She'd faced this years ago. It was just the shock of meeting her rival face to face. 'It's jet lag,' she murmured. 'We only arrived a few hours ago.'

Despite her exhaustion, she hadn't been able to sleep in the vast gold-on-cream bedroom suite she'd been given. She'd felt out of place and on edge, her mind whirring.

'Forgive me, *signorina*, but I think it's more than that.' Dark eyes scrutinised her carefully. It was clear the princess was an astute woman.

Carys released the breath she'd been holding. She couldn't play this charade. She'd never been good at dissembling. She'd rather face facts, however unpalatable.

'Won't you sit down?' Her voice sounded choked.

After a moment the princess took a chair opposite, every movement a study in fluid grace and elegance.

Carys felt like a country bumpkin in her presence. Carefully she locked her hands in her lap to stop them shaking, then drew another sustaining breath.

'The truth is it was a shock to see you.' She paused, watching the other woman tilt her head in curiosity. 'I saw you once with Alessandro, two years ago.'

Pride screamed at her to stop there, to retain her dignity. But despite the craven impulse to keep quiet, Carys refused to play games of innuendo and unspoken secrets. She wasn't that sophisticated. If her blunt unrefined ways didn't fit her husband's milieu, then so be it. If she was going to live here she had to face this.

'I was Alessandro's lover,' she said, her voice stretched thin like fine wire. 'But then I discovered he was planning to marry you.'

There. It was in the open. No hiding from the truth now.

The other woman's mouth sagged and her eyes widened. There was shock in her expression and the taut lines of her neck. Now, this close, Carys wondered if she'd been unwell. She seemed almost gaunt, suddenly fragile rather than chic.

'It was you? I thought there was someone, but Alessandro never said.'

'No.' Bitterness filled her mouth. 'Alessandro kept me very much to himself.'

'But you've got it wrong.' The other woman leaned forward, one thin hand stretched out.

'No, *principessa*. I know exactly how it was.'

'Please. You must call me Carlotta!' There was such tension in her small frame and wide eyes Carys didn't demur. 'And Alessandro and I were *not* planning to marry.'

What? Carys sat bolt upright in her seat, torn from welling self-pity in an instant.

'Nor were we lovers,' Carlotta said. 'Ah, I can see from your expression that's what you thought. But we were never more than friends.'

Carys remained silent. 'Friends' was often a euphemism for something more. Was Carlotta trying to gull her? What reason could she have?

'You must believe me, *signorina*—'

'Carys,' she said abruptly. Formality seemed absurd now.

'Carys.' Carlotta gave her a faltering smile. 'There was no marriage plan, except as a notion put forward between our families. Alessandro's stepmother and my father resurrected the idea. It had been discussed years ago when we were just teenagers, but it never came to anything. Alessandro and I…' She shrugged. 'We grew up together, but there was never that special spark between us. You know?'

Carys knew. The spark Alessandro ignited in her had blazed

like wildfire, instantaneous and all-consuming, incinerating everything in its path. Her doubts, her natural reticence, every defence she had. Oh, but it had been glorious. Heat drenched her chilled body, just remembering.

She looked into the other woman's earnest face. Could it really be true?

'But Livia told me…'

Carlotta nodded. 'Livia promoted the match. She and my family thought a marriage would be in all our interests.'

Something about her diffident tone caught Carys' attention. 'Interests?'

The other woman shrugged one shoulder. 'Business. You know how bad things were after Alessandro's father died. It was touch and go whether Alessandro would lose the company.'

No. Carys hadn't known. She'd guessed things were grim. Had tried to offer support, but the more she'd tried the more he'd turned from her, isolating himself.

'There was talk of a merger, saving Alessandro's company and boosting my family's.' She paused and looked down at her hands. 'Plus I'd been through a difficult time and they thought marriage to Alessandro would save me from myself.'

'I'm sorry. I don't understand.' This was beyond Carys.

Carlotta raised her head and met her gaze squarely. 'I was recovering from anorexia nervosa.' Her liquid dark eyes dared Carys to condemn her, but Carys felt only horror that anyone, much less this beautiful woman, should be struck down by the insidious condition.

'Two years ago I was barely out of hospital. With my family's help, and with Alessandro's, I was just beginning to find my confidence. To go out and even think of starting work again.' She shook her head. 'It took Alessandro's strength and persistence to force me out into society. Even at that worst of times for him, he found time to help me. If it hadn't been for him beside me those first few times, even my parents' support wouldn't have got me out the door.'

'I saw you with him,' Carys found herself saying, 'at a hotel in town. You wore full-length gold. You looked like a fairy princess.' And Carys had never felt more an outsider, standing in the shadows looking in at the glittering world she'd never be part of. At the man she'd lost.

'I remember that night.' Carlotta nodded. 'The gown had to be altered so much. But the full length and long sleeves hid the worst of my condition.'

'I'd never have guessed. You were breathtaking.' Carys sank back in her chair, her head reeling as she digested Carlotta's news.

Was that why Alessandro had seemed so protective? Because he was worried about Carlotta's health? But why had he never said anything to Carys?

'You don't believe me.'

Carys looked up to find Carlotta watching her. 'I do. I just…Livia deliberately let me believe…' The older woman had told her baldly that Alessandro was engaged to marry someone of his own social circle. That he was simply with Carys as a final fling before settling down. She'd even dropped by unannounced with a box of printers' samples for him. It had been full of wedding invitations.

'Livia wanted the marriage quite badly. At one stage it looked as if the company might go under. Which, if you forgive me saying, would impact on her own wealth.'

Livia as a desperate woman? The idea hadn't occurred to Carys. She seemed so assured, so regal, so in control. But perhaps if her position was threatened…

'I heard about the engagement elsewhere too,' Carys said slowly. At the time the evidence seemed insurmountable, especially when Alessandro had refused to explain, merely stating baldly he would never behave so badly and accusing *her* of infidelity! 'I met your cousin, Stefano Manzoni.'

'You know Stefano?'

'Not know, precisely. He took me for coffee and drove me home.' Carys refrained from adding Stefano had viewed her disillusionment with Alessandro as an invitation to sexual dalliance. For all his charm and flattery he'd had more arms than an octopus.

'Ah, Stefano had hopes of that merger. When it became clear it wouldn't happen, he spent a lot of energy aiming for a hostile takeover. But he didn't succeed. He was no match for Alessandro.'

The pride in Carlotta's voice made Carys watch her carefully, but she read no sign of possessiveness. No hint of intimacy in the way she spoke of Alessandro.

'I'm sorry my friendship with Alessandro hurt you. If I'd known—'

'It wasn't you.' Carys leaned forward at the other woman's obvious distress, instinctively accepting what she said as true. It was far more likely that Livia, jealous of her position and eager to shore up the family wealth, had gone all out to scare off an upstart foreigner.

And how little effort it had taken! Carys had been her own worst enemy, only too ready to believe her. The knowledge made her stomach churn in self-disgust and regret.

Alessandro had grown unapproachable, shunning her attempts to comfort him, but if Carlotta was right, he'd never betrayed Carys!

Excitement buzzed through her veins. A crazy delight that he had been loyal to her, though he hadn't loved her. That meant so much.

It meant that though all personal feelings were at an end between them, Carys was marrying a man she could respect.

'But now everything is right between you both,' Carlotta said with such a sweet smile Carys didn't have the heart to disabuse her. 'I'm glad. Alessandro deserves happiness.' She stood, and for the first time Carys noticed the large portfolio resting against her chair. 'And now perhaps we can discuss your gown. I have ideas I hope you'll approve.'

Alessandro replaced the phone with careful precision, a scowl dragging at his brow. The sound of Livia, so rarely flustered, still gabbling her excuses, rang in his ears.

He wasn't in the mood for excuses.

While in Australia he'd been unable to contact his stepmother in person. Frustration had built with each passing day till he'd simply left news that he was bringing home his fiancée and requesting she start the wedding preparations.

It still galled him to discover he'd lived with Carys Wells prior to his accident but hadn't been told about her after his coma. That Livia had kept it from him and told his staff not to refer to the woman who'd been his lover.

As if he needed protecting from his past!

He shot to his feet and paced the room.

Livia's explanations didn't alleviate his thwarted fury at being kept in the dark. It didn't matter that Livia thought Carys on the make, out to snare a wealthy man. Or that Carys had already walked out of his life. Or even that the doctors had said it was best if he were left to recover his memory without prompting.

He should have been told.

Livia's talk of a possible match at the time with Carlotta meant nothing. Alessandro knew without being told what had prompted that—Livia searching for an easy way to shore up the family finances. As if he and Carlotta would ever make a match of it. And, more to the point, as if he'd abrogate his responsibility to salvage the company by buying his way out of trouble with his wife's money!

He rubbed his jaw, realising he now had an explanation for Carys' belief he'd two-timed her with Carlotta. Livia had no doubt blown their friendship out of all proportion.

For a moment he considered enlightening Carys, proving he was innocent of her accusations. But she wouldn't believe him. The distrust flashing in her eyes was too easy to read.

He turned and strode back across the room, unable to ignore any longer Livia's most important revelation.

She'd hinted the affair had been a casual fling, because he'd kept Carys to himself and refused social invitations.

But that only stirred his curiosity. There had been plenty of lovers in his life, yet he'd never been reluctant to take them out publicly. That was one of the functions they performed—company at the many social events he attended.

His skin prickled with preternatural awareness as he remembered Livia saying while Carys was in residence he'd shunned the social whirl, preferring to stay home with his lover. Such behaviour was unprecedented.

And the only reason he could fathom was unthinkable.

That he'd been totally absorbed by her, unwilling to share her with others.

His ability to fixate on what interested him had been one of the keys to his business success. And though he hid it well, his possessive streak was well developed. He hadn't liked to share his toys as a child, and as an adult what he had he held on to.

If he'd felt…attached to Carys, he'd have kept her to himself rather than parade her before the sharks ready to pursue an attractive woman.

If he'd felt attached.

Alessandro shook his head. He didn't do serious relationships. Didn't believe in romantic love. It should be impossible.

Should be.

Yet that frisson of instinct told its own story.

He scrubbed his hand across his jaw, knowing a moment's unfamiliar hesitation.

There were too many unanswered questions, and Carys alone held the key to every answer.

Even his fiancée's relationship with her family puzzled him. Not one of them would attend the wedding. That wasn't like any family he knew.

The woman was an enigma as well as a temptation.

He turned on his heel and strode to the door.

He found her in the grand salon, leaning into the corner of one of the uncomfortable antique sofas Livia had installed.

In her crumpled aqua skirt and matching beaded top, her hair in a ponytail, Carys was a breath of fresh air in the stuffy, formal room.

He walked closer.

She didn't move. Her head rested on one arm as if she'd leaned sideways and fallen instantly asleep. One beaded sandal dangled precariously from her toes. The other lay discarded and his gaze moved to her slim, bare foot, pale and shapely and ridiculously enticing with its painted pink toenails.

A tremor of heat ricocheted through his belly as he followed the lissom curve of her ankle to her calf, her knee and, where her skirt had rucked up, to her thigh.

He remembered the feel of her supple legs encasing him as he thrust her back against the wall of his suite at the Landford. The musky scent of her arousal. The sound of her whimpering mews for more. The sheer erotic blaze of glory that had been him and Carys, on the verge of consummating this…need between them.

Just the echo of that memory had him hard and wanting and ready, feet planted wide and breathing constricted.

Yet instinctively he resisted.

Livia's news made him pause.

It *couldn't* be true that Carys had become so important to him before his accident. He, who'd learnt early not to trust in love or the fidelity of the female sex!

No. There was some other explanation behind his relationship with Carys.

And for the way she made him feel now.

Protective. It was ludicrous. This was the woman he'd told to leave because she'd been with another man. And yet…

Alessandro shook his head, adrift on a sea of turbulent, unfamiliar emotions. He was used to his life proceeding in the pattern he designed. Emotions had no place there. Or they hadn't before Carys.

His shoulders cramped as he fought the tug of feelings, weaknesses, he preferred not to acknowledge.

Despite a few hours' sleep on the long flight from Melbourne, dark smudges were still visible beneath her eyes.

Unwilling concern twisted in his belly.

This woman got to him as no other!

Without giving himself time to think, he bent and scooped Carys into his arms, ignoring the sense of familiarity that rose and crested, like a wave of warmth, as he tucked her close to his torso. Clearly he'd carried her before.

His body knew hers, only too intimately.

He turned for the door. She'd rest better in her own bed. He'd leave her there and then look in on Leo.

Alessandro lengthened his stride as he headed for the main staircase. That time alone with Leo on the flight had whetted his appetite for his son's company. He found the boy more fascinating than any other child of his acquaintance.

Alessandro had reached the top of the stairs when Carys

woke. Her lips parted in a sleepy smile, and heat doused him. Eyes as bright as stars met his and instantly desire exploded into life, tightening his groin, tensing every muscle. In that moment he veered automatically towards the master suite rather than the rooms where she'd been installed.

An afternoon of pleasure, rediscovering her feminine delights beckoned. He quickened his pace.

Then the misty soft smile disappeared, and alarm filled her eyes. Her mouth tightened and she jerked as if trying to wriggle out of his hold.

The heat in his belly fizzed out as quickly as it had ignited. He slammed to a stop. No other woman had ever looked at him in such horror.

'What are you doing?' It was an accusatory gasp. Automatically Alessandro lifted his chin, unaccustomed to such a tone.

'Carrying you to bed. You need rest.'

If anything her tension increased. He felt her stiffen. Her eyes blazed.

'No! I need to see to Leo. He—'

'Our son—' Alessandro paused, savouring the words '—is being looked after by a very capable and pleasant carer.' Carys opened her mouth, to object no doubt. He overrode her. 'In the longer term we will look for a more permanent carer to help with him, but for now be assured he's in safe hands.'

She drew in a deep breath and Alessandro wished he weren't so aware of the soft inviting press of her breast against his chest. It was the most refined torment.

'I can walk from here.'

'But we're almost there.' He stepped forward again, this time towards her guest bedroom. Still he felt her tension. She was stiff as a board, rigid with…anxiety? Distress?

Concern twisted in his belly, a flare of regret for what had happened this afternoon.

'I'm sorry you weren't warned it would be Carlotta coming to discuss your wedding gown today.' He said it slowly, unused to apologising. He'd always prided himself on behaving honourably. 'I only just found out myself.'

It had been Livia's little surprise to confront Carys with the woman she believed had been her rival.

Even now Alessandro found it hard to believe Livia had done anything so crass. He mightn't trust Carys, might have been betrayed by her, but his behaviour and his family's must always be above reproach.

From now on Alessandro would have his personal staff oversee all the wedding arrangements. His stepmother could attend and kiss the bride, but he no longer trusted her with anything more.

'It's all right,' Carys said quickly. 'We had a…useful discussion.' For a moment her gaze clung to his, then she turned her head abruptly, as if dismissing him.

Clearly she didn't accept his apology.

Alessandro registered a curious feeling of emptiness, as if something inside his chest shrivelled. An instant later he put the nonsensical notion from his mind. Resentment stirred at having his word doubted.

'She will do an excellent job,' he said tersely. 'Carlotta is one of Italy's most talented new designers.'

'I'm sure she is,' his bride-to-be said in a hollow voice. 'Her ideas are very clever.'

She sounded as enthusiastic as a woman being measured for her shroud. The idea slashed at his pride.

And this the woman he'd wanted to take to his room and ravish! It shamed him that even now he craved her.

He pushed open her bedroom door and quickly lowered her to the bed, stepping back as if her very touch contaminated.

Separate rooms until after the wedding were preferable after all. Carys needed time to accustom herself to marriage. And he needed space to master these unwanted feelings.

'I'll leave you now to rest.'

Alessandro spun round without waiting for a response and strode from the room.

He didn't see the longing or the anguish in her eyes as she watched him go.

CHAPTER TEN

CARYS drew a deep breath and paused before stepping into the church. The clamour of photographers and sightseers unsettled her, another reminder that she was marrying one of Italy's richest, most eligible men.

Only the presence of Alessandro's security staff kept the eager throng back.

She wished now she'd accepted Alessandro's suggestion that one of his cousins escort her down the aisle.

Foolishly she'd kept alive the faint hope her father would come to give her away. It wasn't a romantic match, but this marriage was for keeps. For Leo's sake. And because once wed she knew Alessandro would never relinquish his wife.

This ceremony would change her life for ever.

Her lips tightened as she smoothed shaky fingers over rich silk skirts. Even after all these years the pain of her dad's rebuff was as strong as ever.

All those missed school plays and speech days where her performances and athletic awards failed to measure up to parental expectations of academic brilliance. She should have realised he wouldn't come, just as her siblings had perfectly sound reasons for not attending, even with Alessandro's offer of free travel. They'd been too busy, promising to visit sometime in the future when life was less hectic.

'Are you ready, *signorina*?' Bruno's familiar husky voice interrupted her reverie. 'Is anything wrong?'

Everything!

She was marrying the man she'd once adored. Not for love, but in a bloodless marriage to keep her son. She had no friends here to support her. She was out of her depth, marrying into an aristocratic world she'd never fit into.

Worst of all, she suspected that despite all that had gone before, she might still…care for Alessandro.

Being with him had awoken so many memories.

More, Carlotta's news that he'd never betrayed Carys, hadn't been unfaithful, had opened the floodgates to emotions she thought she'd eradicated.

He might not love her, but he was essentially the same man she'd fallen for years ago. More impatient, more ruthless, yet just as charismatic and intriguing. And not the lying cheat she'd believed when she'd left him.

Guilt plagued her that she'd believed the worst of him. Her own insecurities had made her too ready to doubt.

Regret gave way to longing, and she found herself wishing this marriage was for real. For love, not expediency.

No! Alessandro wasn't looking for love.

And nor was she.

'*Signorina?*' Bruno stepped close, his tone concerned.

'Sorry, Bruno.' Carys directed a wobbly smile at the bodyguard. 'I'm just…gathering myself. It's a little overwhelming.'

'It will be all right, *signorina.* You'll see. The *conte* will take care of you.'

As he'd taken care of all the wedding arrangements, with a ruthless efficiency that brooked no delay. She was merely an item to be checked off his list.

Acquired: one wife, ditto mother for my son.

Carys repressed a hysterical giggle and lifted her bouquet. The rich scent of orange blossom filled her nostrils, and she swayed, stupidly unsettled by the evocative perfume.

'So he will, Bruno. Thank you.'

She was stronger than this. She didn't do self-pity.

This was for Leo. She had to focus on that. Pushing back her shoulders, she stepped through the door Bruno held open.

Music swelled, the sound of murmuring voices faded, and she was aware of a sea of faces turned towards her. She let her gaze trawl the congregation rather than look down the aisle to where Alessandro stood, waiting to make her his wife.

Pain constricted her chest and she faltered, but curious stares prompted her to move on. They were all strangers, friends of Alessandro. No doubt assessing the bride to see if she lived up to expectations.

Carys lifted her chin, knowing at least she was dressed the part. Carlotta had done a superb job creating a stylish gown that made Carys look feminine and almost elegant.

In grey silk so pale it almost passed for cream, the dress was closely fitted from neck to hips, turning her curves into an almost hourglass figure. From there it flared into lush folds and a rippling train studded with azure beads like hundreds of flashing stars. Long, fitted sleeves and a high collar gave it a severe, almost medieval style, belied by the deep, slit neckline, embroidered with azure sapphires.

The effect was austere yet sumptuous. It was the most flattering, gorgeous thing Carys had ever owned.

She heard whispers as she passed, saw the envy in female eyes, and a tiny thrill of pleasure skimmed her spine.

Now she noticed smiles, one or two familiar faces. And suddenly, there were Alessandro's three female cousins, whom she'd met only two days ago. Accompanied by their husbands and their brood of handsome children. All smiled broadly, nodding encouragement.

They'd chosen pews on the bride's side of the church. Warmth invaded her chilled body at the thoughtfulness of the gesture. It made her feel she wasn't quite so alone.

Then came Carlotta, beaming and gorgeous in ruby red, delight in her dark eyes. And Leo, clapping excitedly and calling to her from his carer's arms. Carys leaned over and gave him a quick cuddle, gaining strength from the flood of love that rose within her.

The buzz of whispered conversation began again and she straightened, feeling the curious stares stabbing into her back. She turned and there was Livia, her fixed smile cool.

This was the woman who'd tried to keep Alessandro and

Carys apart. How would she react if she knew that, despite this charade, they were virtually strangers? That the ceremony was a cruel parody of the dreams Carys had once cherished?

Momentary pleasure faded as reality slammed into Carys. It obliterated her tentative poise and transfixed her with a knife-blade of regret through the chest.

Finally she couldn't ignore any longer the tall man looming before her. Impatience radiated from every superbly tailored inch.

Her fingers clenched on the bouquet as she fought the impulse to run pell-mell back up the aisle and away to freedom. Blood rushed in her ears and her body tensed for flight.

Then he extended one powerful arm, his hand outstretched towards her. She felt his regard like a lick of flame on her face and her body. Her skin prickled in response.

There was no escape. He sucked the air from her lungs and shattered the remnants of her defiant courage.

Like an automaton she stepped forward, letting Alessandro capture her hand. Feeling in that moment the inevitable thrill of energy his touch always evoked.

Yet even that couldn't thaw the chill around her heart.

If only they were marrying for any other reason. If this was about caring instead of custody.

Desolation swept her. If only Alessandro remembered the past, remembered even a little of what they'd shared. But he didn't. Probably never would. Only she recalled the glory as well as the pain, the companionship and the ecstasy and the sense of belonging that had made their relationship unique.

What good were such memories when she couldn't share them? They might as well be figments of her imagination, torturing rather than comforting. She'd never again experience that closeness with the man she was about to marry.

'Carys.' The word feathered across her nerves like the stroke of his hand. His sexy accent invested the name with undercurrents that made her tremble. He turned her towards him and inevitably her eyes lifted to his face.

Her breath caught in astonishment as she met his deep green gaze. Its intensity scorched.

She tried to draw breath, but the incendiary flare in his eyes arrested her. Instead her breathing shallowed, became rapid and unsteady. Her knees trembled and tattered hope rose at what she read in his face.

Alessandro's expression almost made her believe…

The priest spoke and instantly, like a curtain descending to hide a stage, Alessandro's face became blank, wiped of all expression. No heat, no vibrancy, no emotion.

Had she imagined it? Wanted so much to believe he felt something, anything for her that she'd invented that look of fixation and wonder?

Looking now into shadowed dark eyes, Carys felt that tiny seed of hope shrivel in her breast.

The past was the past. What they'd once shared was dead.

In its place she gave herself in a farce of marriage.

Carys tasted the ashes of old dreams on her tongue as she turned to face the priest. Instinct screamed that she was making a terrible, terrible mistake.

But, for the sake of her son, she'd go through with it.

Hours later, drooping with fatigue, face stiff from pinning on a smile, Carys was too weary to object when Alessandro swept her off her feet and into his arms in front of their guests.

'There's no need for pantomime,' she whispered, attempting to ignore the insidious melting sensation as his arms closed round her. 'My legs work perfectly.'

'No pantomime, *wife,*' he murmured as he carried her from the enormous marquee and across the lawn to the sound of applause. 'In Italy men carry their brides across the threshold.'

Carys eyed the hundred metres between them and the villa and kept her lips closed. If Alessandro wanted to indulge in a show of machismo, she had little chance of dissuading him. She'd just have to pretend being held in his arms didn't evoke a cascade of tingling awareness she couldn't control.

She stiffened in his hold.

'You could try smiling,' he said under his breath. 'People expect a bride to look happy.'

Carys bared her teeth in what she guessed was more of a grimace than a smile of joy. The strain of acting the happy bride had taken its toll, shredding her frayed nerves.

'I'm a hotel management trainee, not an actress.'

Not for anything would she let him guess how deeply his embrace affected her. How that terrible gnawing sensation ate once more at her belly, and how her arms ached with the effort not to lift them around his neck so she could sink against the broad cushion of his chest.

'Little viper.' There was no heat in the look he gave her. But there was…something.

Her heart raced faster.

'You can put me down now. We've crossed the threshold.'

He didn't answer, just made for the sweeping central staircase and climbed it with a speed that belied the burden he carried.

Dimly Carys was aware of more applause and laughter from the few staff gathered in the foyer.

But nothing could distract her from the look on Alessandro's face. The determined set of his jaw and the hooded, unreadable expression in his eyes. He was so *focused*.

'Alessandro?'

He didn't answer as he reached the top of the staircase and plunged down a wide hallway.

'My room is to the left.' Was that her voice? That wisp of sound? Her hands clenched together so hard the pulse throbbed through her palms like a beaten drum. Her chest hollowed with an emotion that should have been trepidation.

Ahead wide double doors stood open. Alessandro strode through them then paused to kick them shut with a thud that reverberated right through her.

Slowly the sound died away to echoing silence. A silence taut with rising tension.

Still he held her.

She felt the rise and fall of his chest against her, surely more pronounced than when he'd climbed the stairs.

Did she imagine the shift of those long-fingered hands? The tightening of his embrace, drawing her more firmly against his powerful torso? Heat radiated from him, seeped into her flesh and bones, melting the tightness of her tensed muscles.

Craven, she turned her head, unable to meet his stare. Afraid he might see in her face traces of the crazy yearning that still plagued her. The yearning for *him*. No matter what she'd told herself, she'd never been able to obliterate it.

But she had to hide it.

Her breath hitched audibly as she saw the wide bed that took up one end of the vast room. Canopied in emerald green silk, perfectly centred between French doors that gave on to a balcony overlooking the lake, it took her breath away.

A long garland of roses was strung across the bed head, and rich velvety petals, like a shower of cream and blush and crimson, lay scattered across the sheets.

It looked like nothing so much as…

'Our wedding bed.' Alessandro's deep voice was resonant with an inflection she could almost swear was satisfaction.

Except she knew he had no desire for intimacy. No desire for her. This union was pragmatic, necessary. A legality.

Carys opened her mouth, but no words came. She drew a difficult breath, suddenly aware of how the tight silken bodice cupped her breasts and of the delicate scratch of her new bra's hand-made lace against peaking nipples.

Hot embarrassment flooded her. And more heat that wasn't embarrassment, creating an unsettling, pooling sensation way down low in her womb.

She shifted in his hold, praying he wouldn't notice her traitorous body's reaction to him.

'Your cousins have been busy,' she said in a scratchy, unfamiliar voice. Now she understood the presence of the other women in the house this morning, whispering and laughing over some secret as they made their way upstairs.

She felt the shrug of powerful shoulders. 'Another tradition. It's supposed to bring luck to a marriage. Blessings and, who knows, maybe even fertility.'

Carys wriggled, now desperate to escape. She couldn't keep up this façade of composure. Not when she felt his heart thudding against her, the warm tickle of his breath in her hair and the heat of his hands cradling her.

He made her want things she shouldn't. Things that could never be.

'The union is already fertile. We have Leo. We don't—'

Her words died as, instead of releasing her, Alessandro carried her to the bridal bed. A moment later she was sprawled across the mattress, the rich, sensual perfume of damask roses rising from the petals crushed beneath her.

Automatically she struggled against the encumbering long skirts and the veil dragging her down.

Then she looked up and froze. The expression of feral hunger in Alessandro's face made her heart hammer in her chest. Adrenaline spiked her bloodstream.

She told herself it was from fear. But she didn't believe it.

'You wouldn't condemn Leo to being an only child, would you?'

Alessandro looked down at the woman who was now incontrovertibly *his* and felt a satisfaction such as he'd never experienced.

It outstripped the pleasure of finally wresting the family company back to a secure footing. Even the recollection of his first major business coup, the difficult and astoundingly successful acquisition of a rival manufacturing firm, couldn't match the exultant surge of pleasure that shot through him as he looked down at his woman.

His wife.

It wasn't supposed to be like this. It was supposed to be convenient, sensible, a considered option to safeguard the interests of his son. But right now only his own interests were at the fore of Alessandro's mind.

This week had been a test of endurance such as he'd never known. Time and again he'd reined in the impulse to reach for her and make her his, assuage the physical hunger and, more, the edgy sensation that she could fill the nameless void at the core of his world.

When she'd walked down the aisle, an ice-cool, delicious vision of femininity, his temperature had soared and his libido had leapt into urgent life. It had taken all his resolve to stand and wait, not to throw her over his shoulder and abduct her to someplace private.

Laid out before him like a delicacy awaiting his approval, Carys stoked a fire in his blood for which he knew there could be only one solution.

Sex. Hot and satisfying.

Alessandro drew a slow breath, inhaling the scent of flowers and woman that had haunted him all afternoon.

Damn it. Carlotta had done her job too well. That dress emphasised every sultry line and curve of the woman he'd married. It had driven him crazy from the moment he saw her.

His gaze skimmed the perfect swell of her breasts, hidden yet accentuated by the shadowy V of a neckline that had dragged his attention back again and again. With those scintillating blue stones on the bodice drawing his gaze, he'd spent half the reception ogling his new wife instead of speaking to guests.

When they'd danced he'd put his hands around a waist that was surely too tiny for a woman who'd given birth, and felt a powerful surge of possessiveness overwhelm him.

It didn't matter that he couldn't recall the past between them. It was the present that mattered. Not even his doubts about her trustworthiness impinged on his thinking. Right now nothing mattered more than slaking his desperate lust for his brand new wife.

The self-imposed wait was over at last.

He lifted a hand to his tie and tugged it undone.

'Alessandro!'

His eyes had a glazed look: too intense, too febrile. As if the cool, utterly controlled man she knew had been replaced by a being only half tame. His scar complemented his lawless air. He looked dangerous, rapacious. He'd turned from magnate to pirate in the blink of an eye.

A delicious shiver shot through her, even as she tried to be sensible.

Sleeping with Alessandro would solve nothing. Not when his

heart wasn't engaged. Experience proved she was too vulnerable to him, too hungry for more.

But it's not sleep he wants, purred a demon voice inside her head.

She watched in fascination and dawning horror as his bow tie slid from his neck to the floor. Dark olive fingers flicked open his shirt.

Carys scrabbled backwards on the bed, hampered by the long veil underneath her and the voluminous skirts.

'What do you think you're doing? This wasn't part of our bargain.' If only her voice was strident rather than breathless. Instead it sounded like an invitation.

'Our bargain was marriage, *piccolina.* You're my woman now.' His voice had dropped to a throaty growl that should have warned but instead thrilled her.

She squeezed her eyes shut, seeking the strength she needed.

A dip in the mattress had her eyes popping open to discover Alessandro kneeling astride her thighs, pinning her wide skirt to the bed.

His glittering gaze raked her as if there was no exquisite gown covering her. As if she was his for the taking.

A shiver of pure carnal anticipation ripped through Carys, making a mockery of all her logical protests.

The truth was that, stripped of the varnish of urbane sophistication, Alessandro held an even more potent allure. His untrammelled machismo sent her hormones into overdrive.

'Alessandro.' Her voice was a telltale husky quiver, but she pressed on. 'You don't really want this.'

Or me. Her throat closed convulsively before she could blurt that out.

He'd turned away from her totally once he had discovered Leo. The completeness of his withdrawal, from hot pursuit to cold distance in the blink of an eye, had left her in no doubt she'd been a convenience, easy to use and easy to discard. Of no intrinsic value.

Hot, familiar pain suffused her and she dropped her eyes. She fought against a lifetime's experience of rejection, telling herself she *was* important.

'Not want this?' His words were sharp as the crack of a gun firing. His nimble fingers paused from reefing his shirt undone. 'What are you talking about?'

'You want to make it appear as if we're a real married couple, for the benefit of the guests,' she said in a low, cramped voice, her eyes fixed on his hands rather than his face. 'But carrying me all the way up here did the trick. There's no need to continue the charade.'

'Trick? Charade?' He spoke softly, yet the words throbbed with outrage. 'We are *really* married. You are *really* my wife. And I am now your husband. The *only* man in your life. Remember that.'

'There are no other men in my life.' She wished he'd move. Being caged by his long, lithe, hot body was doing terrible things to her pulse. It throbbed deep between her legs, in the place that suddenly felt so empty and needy. Her lovely dress felt too constricting, the bodice cramping her breath. If only he'd move away.

'And there will be no others from now on. Remember that.'

'I don't need a man in my life.' All she needed was Leo.

'Then you should not have married me, Carys.'

The finality of his tone penetrated, yanking her gaze back to his. Her mouth dried as she looked into his proud, severe, gorgeous face. Clear intent was etched in every angle and curve as well as in the glint of green fire in his deep-set eyes.

'I will not be used as a convenience, Alessandro. We might have married for our son's sake, but you can't have me on tap.' Her jaw ached with tension and she fought to keep her words calm, despite the emotions jangling through her.

'Convenience!' His eyes flared wide. 'You think *this* is convenient?' He snatched her hand up and pressed it, palm down, against his groin.

A massive erection throbbed against her touch. Hot and powerful, it filled her hand. Carys gulped at the memory of all that power unleashed inside her. Need spiralled deep within and she clenched her thighs against the moist proof that he still turned her on as no man ever had.

She tried to pull back, but he wouldn't let her.

Her pulse rocketed as he loomed over her, an autocratic, sexy captor, trapping her with his superior strength. And more, with the raw promise of pleasure in his eyes.

Heat exploded in her belly. The heat of sexual excitement.

She shouldn't want him, but she did. Badly. Despite pride. Despite everything.

'From the moment I saw your photo I've been hard.' He shook his head and she saw a fleeting glimpse of confusion in his eyes. It almost matched her own disbelief at the revelation. He'd wanted her? Not just seen her as a source of information for the memory he'd lost?

Could it be true? Part of her needed to believe that he'd wanted her, even if only on the most superficial level. That she was special to him.

'Hungry for a woman I didn't even know! And in Melbourne…' His eyes flickered half closed as he tilted his body, pushing right into her hold with a jerky thrust that ended in a low masculine groan of need.

The sound aroused her terribly. Memories swamped her of Alessandro gasping out his desire and his pleasure as they melded together in passion. She squirmed beneath him, fruitlessly trying to ease the wanton ache in her womb.

'Do you know what it did to me, letting you go?'

Dumbly she shook her head. He'd seemed so controlled. Yet now, looking into a face drawn tight with barely bridled hunger, a face of pain, Carys began to doubt her certainty.

'For the first time in two years I wanted a woman, but it was obvious you weren't ready. You were exhausted and overwhelmed by the changes in your life.'

He leaned forward, braced on one hand above her, the other hand still clasping her to him. Part of her revelled in his dominance, even as she fought to clear her mind. 'I thought you needed time, Carys. That's why I pulled back.'

For the first time in two years? Her brain stuck on that statement.

She couldn't have heard right. Alessandro was a virile man who revelled in physical pleasure. When all else had bled away, and their relationship grew empty, he'd still been a passionate lover, almost ferocious in his need for her. And in his need to give her equal pleasure.

A shudder of pure longing rippled through her.

'Don't soft soap me, Alessandro. I don't care how many lovers you've had since we were together,' she lied. 'So you don't have to pretend to—'

'Celibacy?' His mouth twisted in derision. 'And what if it's true? What if there's been no one since you?'

Her mind boggled at the idea of Alessandro celibate without her, only feeling desire when he saw her again.

As if his subconscious had kept him for her alone.

No! That was nonsense. The inane imaginings of a woman who'd once been too much in love.

'You can't mean it.'

'You know,' he growled, 'I'm getting tired of you telling me what it is I mean or feel.'

CHAPTER ELEVEN

WITHOUT warning he moved back. Carys was free, her skirts no longer pinned beneath his knees, her hand no longer pressed against that most intimate part of him.

She was relieved. Of course she was. She drew a long, shaky breath. In a minute she'd move and—

Her skirts bunched as strong hands slipped up from her ankles over silk-stockinged calves and knees. By the time Carys collected her stunned thoughts his fingers had reached her thighs, pausing to circle the tops of the stockings Carlotta had insisted she wear with her new underwear and glamorous gown.

Dumbfounded, Carys stared up over a froth of silk to Alessandro's stern face. He was looking down to where his hands played with her suspender straps. Her breath jammed in her lungs at the incredibly erotic sensations his feather-light caresses evoked.

She leaned up, intending to push him away, but it was too late. Already he'd thrust the fabric higher, baring her to his gaze. She felt a waft of air as, with a single tug, he ripped the delicate fabric of her panties away.

The look on his face stopped her instantaneous move to cover herself. Heat sizzled in her blood at the way he stared. Hungry. Possessive. Intense.

The air thickened, making breathing difficult. All she heard was the throb of her pulse, heavy and quick.

The soft wool of Alessandro's trousers brushed her thighs as he knelt between her legs, pushing them wider. Desire exploded as her blood rushed faster in her shaking limbs.

She needed to resist the lure of his seduction. But now, faced with the reality of Alessandro, rampant with desire, her longings obliterated every sensible reason for resistance.

All she could think of was that he hadn't betrayed her. Hadn't taken another lover when they were together, and, if he were serious, not even since they'd parted.

What she'd felt for him hadn't died. It had only been dormant. Even her heartache hadn't killed it off.

'The only thing that would stop me now is if you said you didn't want this.' He lifted his head and pinioned her with his gaze.

She lay supine before the blaze of power she read there, stunned by the immensity of the feelings rising within her.

'Can you tell me you don't want this?'

On the words one long finger slid unerringly through moist folds of skin where she was most vulnerable and sensitive.

Carys shook at the riot of sensations radiating out from his intimate caress. She felt so vibrantly alive. So needy.

Hands in tight fists, she opened her mouth to make him stop, summoning her shattered resistance. But with mind-numbing ease his finger slipped inside, pushing past muscles that clenched hungrily around him.

She almost sobbed with pleasure at the gentle, insistent, seductive slide. Just that alone felt so good. Too good. It had been so long and—

'Carys? I'm waiting for you to tell me.'

From under weighted lids she saw him watch her and felt a flush cover her breasts and cheeks. This was her last chance.

'I…' The tempo of his caress changed, the angle of his touch, and all at once the world shattered around her in a storm of ecstatic energy. She felt it splinter into tiny fragments as she bucked up against his palm, tidal waves of unstoppable sensation radiating out from his touch.

Heat drenched her as the sudden climax, as complete and mind-numbing as any she'd known, blasted her apart.

Only Alessandro's jade gaze held her together. Through the

maelstrom of exquisite delight and overwhelmed senses, his eyes locked with hers. The connection between them sparked like a live wire.

An instant later he moved, surging forward in a powerful motion that thrust her back into the mattress, her legs around his already pumping hips.

Better, so much better than before. The heavy, satisfying length of him filled her completely. His breath was hot at her neck, his broad chest flattening hers, rubbing against her sensitive breasts. His arms curled beneath her and lifted her up so that each rapid thrust slid further and further till surely he touched her very centre.

Her spasming muscles had begun to ease, but now, pummelled by the unstoppable force that was Alessandro, spent nerve endings came abruptly to life again. Hearing him growl her name, feeling his teeth graze her neck at its most sensitive point only heightened the intensity of his raw, earthy loving. Tension spiralled anew as she responded to a passion so primitive she'd never experienced its like before.

The force driving him was so elemental Carys felt as if he branded her for life. She revelled in it.

One last thrust, the slide of eager hands, and she looked up into dazed green eyes as an explosion, more cataclysmic than the first, shook them both.

She heard her name, heard her own high-pitched scream, felt the satisfying hot pulse of his seed inside her as the wave took them, and then they collapsed together.

Alessandro couldn't believe he'd so lost control. One minute they were arguing and the next Carys was tipped up on the bed and he was pounding into her with all the finesse of a rampant stallion.

The sight of her coming apart at his touch, the look of bemused wonder, of yearning on her face, had tipped him over the edge. And shattered every claim he had to be a civilised man.

He had no control where this woman was concerned. Not one iota of subtlety or restraint.

For weeks he'd harnessed a desperate, growing hunger, but

not for a moment had he thought the outcome would be so rough or so barbaric.

Alessandro scrubbed a hand across his face and met his hooded eyes in the bathroom mirror. Even now they glittered with unrepentant satisfaction and excitement. Because Carys, his wife, lay in the next room. In his bed.

He should be ashamed he'd taken her with such unskilled abandon. Yet even that wouldn't stop him a second time.

He reached out for a flannel and turned back towards the bathroom door.

She lay as he'd left her, limp and sated, long legs still encased in stockings and high-heeled satin shoes. The sight of those legs, the rucked up, crumpled dress, and the dark triangle of hair sent a bolt of electricity straight to his groin. His breath whistled out of his lungs as need, instant and consuming, swamped him again.

Had it always been like this with Carys?

Again that tantalising memory teased him, of Carys lying sated in another bed. This time, though, it wasn't her image that caught his attention but the emotions the scene evoked. As if he could feel what he'd felt then. Satisfaction tinged with stirring sexual anticipation. Blatant possessiveness. And…contentment.

It was the latter, the curious sense of absolute rightness, that unsettled him. The suspicion that along with his memory he'd lost something precious.

He'd never responded to another woman so. That made him wary. But he couldn't keep away. Didn't want to.

Already he hungered for her again. This time he'd put her needs first and prove he wasn't a barbaric lout who didn't know how to seduce a woman.

Alessandro avoided her eyes. Heat lashed his cheeks at the way he'd treated her.

She didn't move as he settled himself, naked, on the bed beside her. The dress he'd paid a fortune for was probably unsalvageable, but he didn't care. Didn't care about anything but the hunger thrumming again in his veins like a horde of locusts sweeping down to devour him.

She was barely dozing, worn out by his rough handling. He

should let her rest. She'd been wound tight as a top at the wedding. But in conscience he couldn't let her sleep in her clothes and shoes. She was bound to be uncomfortable and wake.

He reached out and took one slim foot in his hand.

Carys stretched, half aware of something behind her, something moving down her back. But she felt deliciously replete and she clung to sleep.

It was only as hot palms slid against her bare skin that she woke fully.

She lay in bed, still in her wedding gown, and Alessandro had undone each tiny button down her spine. His hands were inside the dress, massaging and soothing so she instinctively arched against his touch.

'You're awake.' His deep voice throbbed with an expression she couldn't identify.

Cravenly she wished she'd woken alone. The memory of what they'd done scoured her brain. The hot musk smell of sex permeated the air, reminding her of how she'd climaxed so easily at his touch. Without even a move to escape!

For all her protests, her fine talk about not being a convenience, she'd succumbed without a fight. Just lay there and given herself up to the ecstasy he wrought.

Carys bowed her head into upturned hands, hunching away from him. What had she done? How could she face herself?

'Carys? Are you all right?' His roving hands stopped, gripping her shoulders beneath her dress.

'I'm fine,' she lied.

She fought the tremors of delight spreading from his touch. The secret excitement hoarded close in her heart that he'd wanted her, and no one else, in all that time. Had she no pride?

It would be too easy to fall in love with Alessandro again. Where would that get her? A one-sided relationship where she gave all and he only as much as it suited him.

But she feared it was too late. That there was no turning back. Emotion filled the bitter void she'd lived with so long.

She needed time to work out what this all meant.

Yet there was no mistaking the sizzle of anticipation in her blood as his hands wandered, evoking magic.

Was she doomed to be enraptured by him all over again?

'Let me help you out of that dress. It can't be comfortable.'

Carys slithered forward out of his reach. 'I can do it myself.' It was too soon to meet his assessing eyes. If she didn't gather her wits, he'd have no trouble reading the effect he had on her.

She made it to the edge of the bed, sitting up and holding the sagging bodice against her breasts with one palm. She stopped there, rigid, as Alessandro walked around to stand before her.

Naked.

Long-limbed, muscle-toned, a tall Adonis come to life.

An *aroused* Adonis.

Her body prickled at nape, breast and forehead as heat bloomed. She swallowed hard and tried to control her wayward pulse.

She'd just experienced the most intense climax of her life. Twice. She should not be interested in sex right now.

He shifted his weight, and she watched, fascinated as muscles flexed in broad thighs and across his taut abdomen. A dart of fire pierced her chest and spiralled lazily down into her womb.

She shut her eyes, trying to banish the heady image of Alessandro, pure potent male, before her. But there was no escape. The picture was branded on her brain.

She tried to think of Leo, of the guests beginning to leave the wedding reception. Of—

'It will be easier if I help, Carys.'

Mutely she sat as he unpinned the veil that hung haphazardly from her hair. She felt the fine lace drop away but didn't open her eyes. Not when Alessandro stood before her so close his heat invaded her space.

His hands at her elbows urged her to her feet and she complied.

She snapped her eyes open, keeping them trained on his shuttered face. What had she expected? To see a reflection of the stunned delight that had consumed her such a short time ago? Instead his hooded gaze and flattened mouth gave nothing away. Only the merest hint of a frown suggested he wasn't quite satisfied with how this had played out.

What more could he want? She'd been putty in his hands, so eager she hadn't even managed to remove her precious gown. Her cheeks burned. She was so easy where he was concerned.

It had always been like that with Alessandro.

'I can take it from there, thanks,' she said in a clipped voice. But as she sidestepped he was already dragging the bodice from her shoulders.

With a shush of silk the dress fell to wedge at her elbows. She darted a look at Alessandro, but, contrary to expectations, he wasn't scrutinising the bare flesh he'd exposed. Instead he watched her face. That look sent her stomach plunging on a rollercoaster ride.

'Let me.' As simply as that, when his hands slipped down her sleeves and tugged, she allowed him to pull the dress away. It dropped in rumpled folds around her feet and he helped her step out. Only now did she realise he'd removed her shoes. She stood before him in bra, suspender belt and stockings. Totally vulnerable.

Yet the glow in his eyes warmed her to the core and stopped her from covering herself.

She felt something swell inside. She felt almost powerful. Felt desired. Even, for a crazy moment, cherished.

'Did you mean that?' Carys found herself asking before she could think twice. 'About there not being anyone since the accident?'

It was so unlikely, especially given his cold fury when he'd accused her of betraying him. But the Alessandro she'd known had never lied. If he said it was so…

He leaned close, holding her with his gaze, and with his hands, large and warm, grasping her upper arms.

For a moment she thought he wouldn't answer. She read a play of unfathomable expressions in his shadowed eyes and felt his fingers stiffen against her bare skin.

Finally he nodded. '*Si.* There was no one.' He didn't look happy about the admission, as if it impinged somehow on his masculinity. But Carys was so elated she barely registered it. A fizzing, as if of a hundred champagne bottles, flooded her bloodstream, making her dizzy. All this time…had he been subconsciously waiting for her?

She tried to blank the preposterous notion from her head, but it lodged there, insidiously tempting.

It meant nothing. He'd been recuperating from injury, or busy with business. Yet a stubborn part of her clung to the idea his celibacy had been because he hadn't had *her*.

'Carlotta told me you hadn't been lovers,' she blurted out. 'She said you hadn't planned to marry her.'

He shrugged, still holding her, yet his face took on a more rigid cast. 'I told you I would not behave in such a way. Carlotta is a childhood friend, nothing more.'

Even now, without remembering the details himself, he was so sure of himself, so positive about his actions!

Carys wished she had half his self-belief. She'd striven a lifetime to overcome the ingrained idea she was second best, fostered by being the 'slow' member of an academically high-achieving family. And by being all but ignored by her busy parents. Even now it was so easy to let doubt take hold.

'I'm sorry I didn't trust you, Alessandro.' Tentatively she raised her hand and pressed it over his where he held her. The feel of her hand on his seemed so right.

It wasn't her fault alone their relationship had unravelled at the seams. But she realised now her readiness to believe the worst, fed by her own sense of inadequacy, as much as Livia's lies, had been a major part of it.

Her throat clogged in mixed hope and fear as she waited for his response. Tension buzzed her rigid body.

'Now you know the truth,' he said dismissively. 'The past doesn't matter.'

But it does, she wanted to cry as pent up feelings lashed her. If they'd been able to trust, to believe in each other, they might still be together. Truly together, not yoked in a marriage of convenience.

Bitterness welled on her tongue as regrets swamped her.

'I believe you didn't betray me, Alessandro. Is it so hard for you to believe I didn't betray you?'

Alessandro stared down into her earnest, flushed face and felt again the stab of unfamiliar emotion in his gut. This woman twisted him inside out. With her words as well as her delectable body.

Automatically he shied from the emotions she sought to awaken. They were too confronting, too foreign to a man who built his life on logic and self-sufficiency. Too dangerous.

'I believe, *piccolina*, that the past is the past. There is nothing to be gained in revisiting it. Instead we have our future with our son to create. Our future together.'

She blinked and he could have sworn he saw tears well in eyes that had turned from hopeful blue to dull slate-grey in a moment. Heat corkscrewed through his chest at the knowledge he was responsible. But he refused to lie, even to placate the woman he intended to live with for life.

His trust only went so far. Taking any woman's word without proof was as foreign to him as breathing underwater.

She could not seriously ask him to accept, on the word of a woman he couldn't remember, that he'd been wrong to accuse her of infidelity. He must have had excellent reasons for the accusations.

Until he knew more, he would reserve judgement. Any sane man would.

Carys shifted, trying to shrug off his hold.

'I need to hang this dress up.' Her voice was as cool and colourless as a mountain stream and she avoided his eyes.

Though she didn't berate or accuse, he felt her disappointment as a tangible force. His belly clenched with a sensation that might have been regret.

Alessandro didn't like it.

'Later.' The word emerged roughly, dragging her stunned gaze to his face.

Didn't she understand that he gave her as much as any man could in the circumstances? That he'd already gone out on a limb tying himself to a woman he didn't know simply for the sake of their son?

And for the shimmering inexplicable force that hovered between them.

No! Now he was buying into that female territory where emotions rather than sense ruled the world.

'This is more important than your dress.' His hands slid round her bare shoulders and he yanked her close, revelling in the bare heat of her torso, the delicate scratch of her lace bra and soft breasts against his thudding chest.

Without giving her time to protest he covered her mouth with his, taking advantage of her parted lips to thrust inside and claim her. She tasted of hot summer days, sun-ripened cherries and warm, luscious woman.

This was real, tangible. The attraction between them sizzled and snarled like a live current. He sank into her sweet depths with something suspiciously like relief. One hand splayed in her hair, holding her so he could ravage her mouth. The other pressed her close.

Hunger rose, raw and untrammelled, making a mockery of every resolution to remain in control. Need consumed him.

Dimly he was aware he'd unleashed an onslaught on her, not a slow seduction. But he couldn't stop, couldn't think, until gradually the rigidity left her bones and she melted into him, her hands sliding up to cup his neck. He shuddered with pleasure when she pressed into him as if she too couldn't get enough of the powerful passion driving them.

Only much later, when their chests heaved from lack of oxygen and her lax form told him she was his for the taking, did he remember his vow to seduce and not simply ravage.

Moments later he'd flicked her bra open and dragged it off. He bent and cupped one luscious breast in his hand. Its weight was perfect, made for his palm. She sighed as he closed his lips around one peak and suckled, cried out when he bit gently on her nipple. Her hands dug into his skull, keeping him close as he lavished attention on one breast then the other. And all the while his body clamoured for more.

She swayed in his hold and he nudged her back a step till she collapsed on the bed. Perfect. Before she could protest he was between her knees, shoulders spreading her thighs, his hunger an unstoppable force.

'I—' Her words died as he cupped her with his palm, gently applying pressure till he felt a response shudder through her. He nudged aside her hands that had sought to stop him. Then he took his time, stroking and teasing till her body lifted off the mattress to meet his hand.

Relief scoured him. She was as needy as he. As hungry for this passion. His body felt gripped by a vice, too tight, too hard, too impossibly aroused, just by the sight and sound of Carys responding to his ministrations.

Never had a lover's pleasure affected him so profoundly. He wanted to give her more and more, even as his whole being thrummed with the need for release.

'Alessandro!' Her protest died as he parted her folds and licked her, tasting the dewy salt tang that was pure Carys. It was addictive, as was the delicate shiver of her legs enfolding him.

It didn't take much to push her over the edge and he revelled in the sound of her gasping breath, the feel of her body curving up around him, the shudders racking her from top to toe. He smiled his satisfaction even as he forced down a desperate hunger for his own release.

He needed to show Carys that here, now, was the beginning of their life together. That it was more important than the past she clung to and that he couldn't recall.

That yawning blank disturbed him more than he'd admit, but he was determined to carve a life with his child. And, therefore, his bride. He wanted to please her, sate her, till she was completely, absolutely *his*. Till she didn't hanker for anything else. So Carys understood the magnitude of this passion between them.

And gave up badgering him with emotions and tests of trust.

What they had was enough. More than enough.

Carys surely would attest to that as he brought her to climax again. This time he leaned over her, watching her eyes shine like a starry night.

Then, only when she was spent, did he slowly join with her, careful of her exhausted body. He trembled, almost undone by the depth of pleasure at being inside her. She tugged him close and held him to her. Instantly desperate energy rose and swamped him. He gave up all pretence at control and lost himself in the ecstasy of being at one with his wife.

Impossibly, it was as good as before. Better.

He didn't understand.

But he ceased thinking as Carys wrapped her legs around his hips and told him exactly how much she wanted him.

Aeons later Alessandro's drumming heartbeat slowed and he recovered enough to roll his weight off Carys and pull her onto him. Only then did his brain engage.

Despite the incredible pleasure they'd shared, his thoughts were nothing but trouble.

Above all was the niggling, astonishing idea that sex with Carys felt too good to be just about physical release.

That it felt profoundly important.

Like coming home.

CHAPTER TWELVE

'PAPA! Papa!' Leo's screams of delight resounded in the glassed-in room that housed the villa's full-length pool.

Carys looked up from her paper to see Alessandro rise out of the water like a sleek, mighty sea god, all honed muscle and heart-stopping virility. The kick of her heartbeat accelerating played havoc with her breathing.

Every night since their wedding Carys had shared a bed with him. She hadn't been able to resist. She'd learned again the feel, scent and taste of that superbly sculpted body. Learned too the passion and pleasure he could unleash in her. Yet familiarity with his magnificent body didn't lessen the intensity of her reactions. Just the sight of Alessandro, almost naked in low-slung swimming trunks, set a pulse thrumming deep in her womb.

With casual ease he threw Leo in the air then caught him again, spinning him round, toes dragging in the warm water. Leo squealed with glee, holding tight to Alessandro's sinewy forearms.

Her son. Her husband.

A flash of heat speared Carys at the sight of them together, delighting in each other's company.

Stupidly, emotion clogged her throat.

Alessandro and Leo were developing the sort of relationship she'd dreamed of for her son. At first Alessandro had been wary, almost diffident, as if dealing with a baby was tantamount to meeting an alien being. But gradually he'd become adept at handling his child and a camaraderie had begun to build between them, a relationship that was based on far more than duty.

She knew about that sort of relationship. Initially she'd feared that, though Alessandro had been adamant he wanted his son, adamant enough even to marry *her,* he'd be the sort of parent she'd suffered. The sort who provided the necessities of life, and even some of the comforts, but never quite connected with their child. The sort who saw parenting as an obligation, especially when their child was a cuckoo in the nest, unlike them or their other offspring.

'Papa!' Leo's voice grew shriller as he demanded another aerial stunt.

Carys lowered her newspaper and turned more fully towards the pool, looking over her glasses. That high-pitched tone was a sure sign that Leo was tired and over-stimulated by this exciting new game. If it continued he'd end in tears.

She opened her mouth to warn Alessandro and suggest it was time to finish, but he forestalled her. He lowered Leo into the water and gently towed him along, pointing out the richly coloured sea creatures featured at the bottom of the enormous mural covering the end wall. After a few grizzly moments Leo became intrigued, leaning forward in his dad's arms and trying to repeat some of the words.

Carys leant back. Alessandro really was developing an understanding of his son. It was there in his eyes when he looked at Leo, in the calm encouragement and occasional firm reprimands he gave. He had a natural aptitude for parenting.

He enjoyed being with Leo. Why else would he spend so much time here at the villa, ignoring the lure of the office?

Alessandro still drove himself, working long hours, but increasingly those hours became flexible. Today he'd arrived mid-afternoon, at a time when Carys and Leo were always in the pool. Instead of closeting himself in his office or taking important calls, he'd spent the last half hour in the water with Leo.

She'd done the right thing. Leo and Alessandro were building something that would last a lifetime. Respect and love. The sort of relationship she'd longed for as a kid. The sort she'd vowed her son would have. Now he'd have it with both parents.

Even if all that kept those parents together was their child. And lust.

She grimaced, ashamed to admit the all-consuming hunger Alessandro sparked in her.

The lust would fade, on Alessandro's part, at least. Carys was a novelty still, and she was here, available, all too ready to accede to his every sensual demand.

Heaven help her when he lost interest in her!

For with every day spent here in his home, every night cocooned in his arms, sated from his lovemaking, Carys felt the tendrils of her old feelings bud again. She tried to resist, to remind herself that what she felt wasn't reciprocated, that this was a marriage of convenience.

The trouble was it *felt* like more.

She squeezed her eyes shut, pinching the bridge of her nose, reminding herself she'd given up on self-delusion.

She'd made her decision: to settle for a loveless marriage. To settle for what was best for Leo.

It didn't matter that deep inside she knew 'settling' meant accepting second best, accepting the sort of inferior status she'd fought against all her life. 'Settling' felt dangerously like slicing her innermost self apart, day by day. Till one day, perhaps, there'd be nothing of the real Carys left, just the façade of a woman who was nothing more than Leo Mattani's mother and Alessandro Mattani's wife.

She couldn't allow herself to think like that!

Clearly she'd made the right choice. Seeing Leo and Alessandro together made that obvious.

It didn't matter that she still secretly yearned for—

'Carys?' Alessandro's deep voice slid over her like the caress of warm hands on bare flesh.

She looked up to discover him standing before her, legs planted wide in an assured stance that spoke of masculine power. In his arms Leo smiled down at her.

'Mumum.'

Carys thrust her newspaper and reading glasses aside and held her hands out for Leo. After a quick glance, she avoided Alessandro's penetrating stare. Sometimes, as now, his regard was so intense it felt as if he delved right inside her.

'Here, sweetie.' She cuddled Leo close when Alessandro passed him to her, undoing her towelling robe and wrapping it around him, rubbing him dry. 'Did you have a good time?'

Leo grinned sleepily, his eyelids already drooping. 'Papa.' He turned and waved an arm at Alessandro.

'Yes, you swam with papa, didn't you?'

For the life of her Carys still couldn't meet her husband's hooded green gaze. There'd been a hint of something far too unsettling in it. She felt it flick over her, tangible as a touch.

Carys repressed a shiver of unwanted awareness and concentrated on drying Leo.

'It's time Leo had his nap,' she said eventually, sliding forward on her seat, ready to stand. Hopefully once she was in Leo's room the trembling eagerness for Alessandro's touch would abate. If she stayed any longer Alessandro would surely pick up on her edginess and guess the cause. When it came to understanding the demands of her body, he had more expertise than she!

'I just called Anna on the house phone. She'll be here in a minute to collect him and put him down for a rest.'

Carys frowned as Alessandro scooped Leo from her arms.

'I can settle him.'

Broad shoulders shrugged. 'We pay Anna to help with Leo. Let her do this while you finish reading. See? Leo's happy.'

He was right. Leo was calling out to Anna as she entered the room. There was no logical reason for Carys to insist on settling Leo herself. To do so would only arouse Alessandro's curiosity. Besides, as soon as Leo left, so would Alessandro. No doubt he'd taken enough time away from his work.

'OK,' Carys said at last, smiling to Anna and waving to Leo. Her heart swelled when Leo blew her a smacking kiss as he was carried from the room.

Her son was so happy here. She *had* done the right thing.

Carys eased back in her seat and picked up her newspaper.

It was only as she rested her head on the lounge that she realised Alessandro hadn't moved. He stood a few metres away, watching her.

Heat crawled up her throat and across her breasts. She realised her robe was wide open where she'd snuggled Leo and quickly closed it, knotting the belt tightly. There was something too unsettling about Alessandro's regard.

Instead of leaving, he took the lounge beside hers. Yet he didn't lean back to face the pool, and beyond it the manicured garden and lake. He sat sideways, facing her.

Too close! Far too close!

Those shivery little tremors inside Carys intensified, as did the hollow sensation in the region of her pelvis. He only had to look at her and desire consumed her. The realisation made a mockery of her hard-won self-control.

She searched for something to break the silence that felt too weighty for comfort.

'I haven't seen much of Livia since the wedding.' Carys could have kicked herself as soon as the words were out, for the last thing she wanted was to talk about her mother-in-law, or suggest she wanted to see more of her.

The relationship between Carys and Livia was polite and stiffly cordial, no more. Carys saw no point in confronting her about her lie that Alessandro had intended to marry Carlotta, but nor could she forget the way the older woman had deliberately misled her.

Alessandro's brows rose. 'Livia has been…busy lately.'

Carys paused, digesting the curious inflection in his tone. It sounded almost like disapproval. Alessandro and his stepmother weren't particularly close, but they had always seemed to get on.

'Really?'

'Yes.' This time there was no mistaking the spark of anger in Alessandro's eyes or the firming of his jaw. Had there been a falling out between him and Livia? Had he finally grown tired of her snobby, manipulative ways? It was too much to hope for. 'She has commitments elsewhere.'

Carys would have to be blind and deaf not to notice the

warning in his tone, but she refused to back off. She knew to her cost just how much damage Livia could do. She needed to understand what was happening.

'You said she'd come to advise me on how to play the role of *contessa*.' Carys was proud of the way she kept the bitterness from her voice. Of course she needed to learn, but the implication that she was so way below standard still hurt.

His gaze narrowed and he sat straighter, shoulders seeming to broaden before her eyes. 'You're not playing a role, Carys. You *are* the Contessa Mattani. Remember that.'

'Oh, I'm hardly likely to forget.' Surrounded by luxury acquired by the Mattani family over generations, Carys felt like an intruder, an impostor. She still couldn't get used to having servants at her beck and call.

Sometimes as she walked past the family portraits in the upstairs gallery, she felt the accusing eyes of long dead Mattanis, as if they wondered how someone as ordinary as she came to be in their home.

Carys shook her head. She had to get out of this place. She was going stir crazy.

She hadn't ventured out of the grounds in the weeks since the wedding, too busy ensuring Leo settled in to his new home. And with the memory of paparazzi surrounding the church on her wedding day, too nervous to face the press on her own. Alessandro hadn't offered to take her out, but nor had she expected him to. She had no illusions about her place in his life.

'Don't worry, Livia will perform the responsibilities of the Contessa Mattani until you're ready to take over.' The steel in his eyes made her wonder if she'd have to pass some test to convince him she was ready. Obviously he doubted her ability to make the grade. 'But I think it better if someone more compatible and…reliable is your mentor in the meantime.'

Reliable? It sounded as if dear Livia had blotted her copy book. Carys was human enough to feel a surge of satisfaction at the thought of the woman's schemes coming undone just a little.

'Who did you have in mind?' For one electrifying moment she thought he was going to take on the role himself.

Then common sense returned. Even as his wife she wouldn't merit that much claim on Alessandro's time.

'I thought perhaps Carlotta.' He sat back, watching her reaction.

'Carlotta?' Carys felt relief sweep her. 'I'd like that.' After the initial stiffness they'd got on well. Carys was attracted to the other woman's honesty and dry wit. She'd enjoy spending time with the princess. 'As long as that's OK with her,' she added diffidently.

'I'm sure it will be. She's already mentioned the idea of coming to see you.'

Carys frowned. 'But I haven't heard from her.'

Alessandro leaned forward a fraction, elbows on thighs and hands between his knees. 'No doubt she was allowing the newly-wed couple time alone before making social calls.'

Carys looked dumbfounded at his words. As if the idea of a honeymoon period was a foreign concept.

Alessandro felt frustration rise again. No matter how hot and heavy their lovemaking, afterwards Carys somehow managed to put a distance between them. Just as she'd done since he'd arrived at the pool today.

Of course he didn't want her hanging on his sleeve, pretending to dote on him, but the perpetual distance between them whenever they were out of the bedroom annoyed him.

He wanted…

He didn't know quite what he wanted. But it was definitely not a wife who treated him like a polite stranger unless he was naked and inside her. *Then* she responded with all the enthusiasm he could wish for.

Fire ignited in his groin and spread, tightening thighs and buttocks, curling fingers into fists and drawing the tendons in his back and neck unbearably taut.

Just thinking about sex with Carys made him hard. While she sat there, cool as a cucumber, quizzing him about Livia!

He'd thought marriage would bring respite from the surge of hormones that made him crave Carys like a fire in his blood. Yet the more he had her, the more he wanted her. And not just in bed.

Even watching her pull her robe open to nestle their son against her breast as she dried him made Alessandro rigid with desire.

What did that say about him?

He scrubbed a hand over his jaw, trying to ease the escalating tension there.

She didn't even dress provocatively to entice him. Despite the massive injection of funds to her new bank account, she still wore the simple, cheap clothes she'd brought with her.

There were no designer gowns or expensive shoes. No new handbags or hairstyles. Not even sexy new lingerie. Each night he found himself discarding her plain cotton night shirts. She didn't even bother to acquire a skerrick of lace or silk to entice her husband.

And somehow he still found her more alluring than any silk-clad siren of his memory.

Swaddled in thick towelling, her hair drying around her shoulders, and her face washed clean of make-up, Carys made his heart thud faster and his libido claw for release.

He told himself he'd come home to spend time with Leo, and he *had* enjoyed his son's company. Young Leo had an energy and an enquiring mind as well as an open, loving disposition that made him a pleasure to be with. Yet Alessandro had been distracted time and again by the enigmatic woman at the poolside. She'd been so engrossed in her reading it was clear her husband didn't hold her interest.

He didn't understand her.

'You haven't been away from the house,' he found himself saying.

She angled her chin a fraction, in that unconscious gesture of defiance he found ridiculously appealing.

'I didn't want to brave the press. I'm not used to that sort of attention.'

Guilt punched him. Why hadn't he thought of that? He'd been so busy adjusting to his ready-made family while trying to maintain his usual constant work schedule, it hadn't occurred to him.

'I'll arrange for a quick photo opportunity in the next few days. We'll give them a chance to snap shots of the happy couple.' He paused on the thought of how inappropriate the phrase seemed. 'Then the pressure will ease. Tell the staff when you want to go out and security will be arranged. You need have no fear. You'll be well taken care of.'

'Thank you.'

Again she avoided eye contact. Frustration returned. He felt an unfamiliar desire to provoke a reaction, any reaction from her. He refused to be ignored.

'The staff can tell you the best places to shop. No doubt that's high on your agenda.' After all, she now had a substantial fortune to spend.

Cool grey eyes met his as she frowned. 'Why would I need to shop? Do you mean for an outfit to wear for this press session?' She shook her head. 'There's no need. Carlotta already had two extra outfits made for me, a suit and a dress. I'm sure one of them will do. They're both lovely.'

Alessandro waved a dismissive hand. 'No doubt whatever Carlotta provided will be suitable. But you'll want to start enjoying your money and buy a new wardrobe.' On his instructions one of his secretaries had already provided her with a card linked to her new bank account.

Carys sat back in her seat, her brow clearing. 'There's no need. I've got plenty to last me till the cooler weather comes. Then I'll have to invest in a new winter coat.'

'A new winter coat?' His voice trailed off. Winter was months away. Summer was just starting. Who did she think she was fooling? 'With all that money at your disposal you expect me to believe you have no interest in spending it?'

'I know you're providing money for expenses, but—'

'Money for expenses!' This woman was something else. She reduced her new-found wealth to the status of grocery funds. 'It's far more than that, Carys. Remember, I know exactly how much since I'm paying it.'

'There's no need to sound so accusing.' A flash of fire in her eyes sent shards of ice-hot need splintering through him. That only intensified his anger.

'And there's no need to pretend your outrageously lavish allowance is a mere pittance.' The games women played!

Carys stiffened, looking more like an ice queen than the ordinary working girl he'd plucked from drudgery. 'I don't know what you're talking about.'

Alessandro shot to his feet, trying to work off his anger at her games by pacing the length of the pool and back. This pretence was the sort of thing he abhorred. Next she'd be complaining the funds he provided weren't enough.

'Of course you know. You read the prenup in such detail you must have checked every word twice. You have enough money in your personal account now to keep you in Gucci, Versace and Yves Saint Laurent every day of the year.'

Clouds must have passed over the sun, giving the illusion she'd paled.

Then, as he approached, Alessandro saw the way her hands gripped the arms of her chair, the stiffness in her small frame as she sat up. And in her eyes, what looked like shock.

'You're kidding.' Even her voice sounded different. Light and breathless. 'Why would you do that?'

He shrugged, refusing to put into words the suspicion that without such a financial incentive, she might one day walk out on Leo. And him.

'You need to dress as befits my wife.' Even to his own ears it sounded unconvincing. 'But you know all about it. You signed the agreement before we married. That set it all out.'

The sight of her gaze sliding guiltily from his, the way her hands tightened even more till they resembled talons clawing at the padded chair arms, brought him up short.

Instinct honed over years of business dealings told him something was wrong. Something important. The hairs at his neck rose and he stilled.

'Yes. Yes, I signed it.'

Alessandro's gaze strayed from her mouth, distorted as she bit hard into her bottom lip, to her knees, now pressed up to her chest. She looked so *vulnerable*. What on earth?

Eventually he followed the direction of her stare, to her folded newspaper and glasses. It was a prestigious English-language paper, open at the international news. He recognised the large picture of the United Nations Secretary General in one corner.

The same page she'd been reading over half an hour ago when he'd arrived.

'Carys?' He took a step closer till she turned to face him. Her expression was closed, rigid with something that looked like fear.

'What is it?' He glanced again at the newspaper. It was impossible that, even with the noise in the pool distracting her, it could take so long to read a single page.

Then he remembered the way Carys had hesitated over some passport control forms as they'd travelled.

'You *did* read the prenup,' he said to himself as much as her. 'I saw you.' He watched her swallow, almost wincing as the motion looked so difficult.

'I…started to.' Still she didn't face him. 'But in the end I decided it was just saying I'd get nothing of yours if we divorced.' She lifted her shoulders in a jerky shrug. 'So I signed. I didn't know anything about a big allowance.'

'Liar,' he whispered. 'I saw you. You were reading the last page just before you signed.'

Her head whipped around and he saw high colour flag her cheeks. Yet her face was chalky pale.

An appalling notion smote him. An unbelievable one.

'You *can* read, can't you?'

Had she been sitting there all this time, pretending to examine an article that made no sense? His stomach plunged heavily as an alien emotion kicked him hard.

'Of course I can read!' She drew herself up straighter in her chair, eyes brilliant with fury. 'How do you think I did my job if I couldn't read? Just because I…'

'Just because you…?' Alessandro stepped forward to stand before her, hands planted akimbo.

He watched her wrap her hands around her bare legs, rocking forward in the age-old motion of someone seeking comfort.

'I didn't read your precious papers.' She almost spat the words at him, they came out so fast. 'I began to but I was exhausted and stressed and…' She paused so long he thought she wouldn't continue. 'And I have dyslexia,' she said on a surge of breath. 'That's why I wear tinted glasses; they help me focus. But sometimes, especially when I'm tired or when the text is a solid mass, it's almost impossible to read, because whole lines keep disappearing and the words turn into a jumble. Legal papers are the worst.'

Silence. A silence ringing with the echo of her defiant tones.

Alessandro's heart twisted in his chest as he saw what it had cost her to share the truth. He wanted to reach out and soothe the hurt so evident in her drawn features, but guessed his touch wouldn't be welcome.

Her lips trembled into a heart-wrenching parody of a smile. 'It's not something I tell many people about.'

'But you told me, didn't you? When we were together before?' He knew it, sensed it, even though he didn't remember.

'I… Yes. You knew. Of course you did.'

Of course he did.

They'd been that close, sharing secrets as well as passion. Once again Alessandro had that sickening sense of taking a step straight into a yawning abyss. His damned memory loss had robbed him of so much. Robbed them both.

He took a deep breath, trying to make sense of what Carys had revealed.

'But you're reading the international news page.' In a paper renowned for in-depth, incisive journalism. It was no lightweight read.

Carys moved so swiftly, surging to her feet, that he stepped back a pace. Her eyes glittered blue fire as her gaze clashed with his.

'Just because I'm a slow reader doesn't mean I'm thick! You understood that before.' She paused, as if grappling for control over her hurt and disappointment.

Why couldn't he have remembered this one thing at least about her?

'I read the international news because I'm interested, even if it takes me longer than some people. Some days, like today, it's just slower than others, OK?'

'OK.' Alessandro watched the fire dim in her eyes as she wrapped her arms tight round her torso again.

Guilt carved a hole inside Alessandro's chest as he remembered how he'd all but forced her to sign the prenup on the spot. He'd already guessed she was exhausted and wrung out from stress. He'd had no compunction about seizing on her weakness and stampeding through her objections to get what he wanted, just as he would in any business deal.

But this wasn't business. It wasn't nearly so simple.

'I'm sorry,' he murmured, watching her rub her arms as if from cold. Clearly her dyslexia was an emotional issue. She was so defensive. 'I didn't mean to imply—'

'That I'm dumb?' Her lips curved up in a smile that held pain rather than humour.

'Of course not. No one would.' He didn't have any personal experience of the condition, but even he knew that.

Her laugh was hollow. 'You think not?'

'Carys?' Her distressed expression was too much. He reached out and took her by the shoulders. 'Talk to me,' he commanded as he massaged her stiff muscles, trying to ease their rigidity. Her pain made him feel uncomfortable…edgy…protective.

Again that bleak smile. 'Everyone thought I was slow-witted because I couldn't read well. *Everyone.* I was always bottom of the class. Even when I reached high school and a teacher suspected what was wrong, it was easier for people to think I was just slow.'

Alessandro frowned. 'Kids can be cruel.'

She lifted her shoulders in a weary gesture. 'Not just kids. My father is a professor; my mother ran her own business. My siblings are all academic over-achievers. They found it difficult to adjust to me. I didn't measure up.'

'Adjust to *you?*' Alessandro's jaw tightened. 'They should have been encouraging you, looking after you.'

She shook her head. 'They preferred to bury themselves in their own activities.' From the raw pain in her voice Alessandro guessed they had provided precious little support.

The idea infuriated him. Kids needed more from their parents than the bare necessities of life.

Suddenly it struck him that he and Carys had a lot in common— both had been left at too young an age to look after themselves.

'Even when I stopped working in dead-end jobs and finally found the nerve to sign up for a hotel management degree, they saw it as second best.' She paused, the dead chill in her eyes carving a chasm through his chest. 'That's all they ever expected from me…second best.'

'Carys.' He pulled her close, pushing her head down against his shoulder. His heart thumped unsteadily at the wild emotions running through him. He'd been angry and distrustful of her, yet now, seeing the hurt she tried so hard to hide, he felt compassion and a driving need to make things better.

Her pain felt like his. Sharp as a blade, it transfixed him.

He'd never experienced such empathy for anyone else. Or such a strong impulse to protect.

Automatically he rocked her against him, feeling shudder after shudder rack her taut frame.

'You're not second best, Carys. You're a wonderful mother. Anyone seeing Leo would know that. Plus you excel at your work.' He'd taken the time to find that out in Melbourne. 'And you haven't let dyslexia hold you back from tertiary study.' How she'd coped with that he had no idea. His own ability to read and quickly absorb huge amounts of information was something he'd always taken for granted.

'You're a special woman, *tesoro*. Never forget it.'

Slowly he stroked her back, feeling her tension begin to ease. But he didn't release her. He wanted to hold her. And not just because she was the woman at the centre of every erotic daydream he'd had for months.

He wanted to comfort her. The tenderness and regret that welled inside him at her story, the tide of anger on her behalf, overwhelmed him.

His mind shied from the realisation that he'd so easily misread her. Because if he dwelled on that too long, he might have to consider that he'd misjudged her in other things.

Her question on their wedding night echoed too clearly for comfort.

I believe you didn't betray me, Alessandro. Is it so hard for you to believe I didn't betray you?

CHAPTER THIRTEEN

ALESSANDRO nuzzled the silk tresses on his pillow, inhaling the scent of flowers. He wound a strand round his fingers, then brushed the end across her bare breast.

Carys shivered. Even now, exhausted from lovemaking, she responded to him. As he did to her.

It was as if she'd got into his blood, his bones.

Still it wasn't enough. 'Tell me about us,' he murmured, finally confronting the need that had gnawed at him so long. 'What did we do together…before? What was it like?'

He watched her breathing falter. Raising his gaze, he found her biting her lip. Wary eyes met his.

'You really want to know?'

He nodded. More than ever he needed to understand. Knowing the past might help him understand the present.

Huge eyes surveyed him carefully, as if seeking a hidden trap. Then she looked down to where he caressed her. Long eyelashes shielded her eyes from his gaze.

'It was like a summer storm. Like a lightning strike out of the blue.' Her lips tilted up. 'It was sudden and overwhelming. Wonderful and scary and…undeniable.'

'The sex, you mean?' She described perfectly the marrow-melting intensity of their loving.

Her moue of disappointment told him he'd got it wrong. 'No.' She tugged the sheet up, dislodging his hand. He ignored the tiny splinter of hurt that jabbed him.

'So tell me. What did we do together?'

She shrugged. 'Everything. You taught me to ski and snow-board. We went climbing and hiked some of the hills here. I cooked you Aussie style roast lamb and pavlova for dessert, and you taught me about Italian wines and the history of the area.' Her voice was so wistful he felt a pang of discomfort.

But greater still was his confusion. He'd taken her climbing and hiking? He slid a hand around her hip, lodging her concretely against him as the world started to spin.

'Alessandro? What is it? Have I sparked a memory?'

Numbly his shook his head. 'No memory.' The words were curt, but he couldn't help it. He still couldn't face with equanimity the fact he'd probably never remember.

Yet that wasn't what shocked him.

Climbing, hiking, constituted his rare, private time away from the high-pressure business world. He climbed with a friend or two. Male friends. He hiked alone. Always. Most of his acquaintances had no notion he loved the mountains even more than his fast cars. The idea of sharing that most precious private time with a woman was astonishing.

'We hiked together?' His voice sounded rusty.

Carys nodded. 'It was glorious. The countryside's so lovely. In the evening we'd sit together and discuss where we'd head the next weekend.'

'Really?' The picture she conjured was completely foreign. Yet it seemed…right. He frowned, wondering how he knew that so definitely when he remembered nothing.

'You don't believe me.' She shuffled away to prop herself against the bed head, hurt shimmering in her eyes.

He reached out to cup her face, stunned by what he'd learned. He needed to know more. But this wasn't the time.

'I believe you, Carys.' He paused. 'Tell me about Leo. What was he like as a newborn? Did you know from the first how intelligent he was?'

The sound of his son's laughter warmed Alessandro, but it was the sight of his wife, smiling as she held Leo up to look out the ferry window, that made something shift inside him. Something he hadn't ever acknowledged before.

The barrier that had kept him safely separate and self-contained from those who tried to get too close.

Alessandro drew a slow breath and exhaled, battling the turmoil inside.

This shift wasn't a sudden event. The barrier had been crumbling for weeks. Day by day the connection with Leo and Carys had strengthened, growing into something he'd never expected to feel. There was protectiveness, possessiveness, caring. Joy and acceptance.

Despite the ferry's smooth progress across the lake, Alessandro rocked back on his feet as if struck off balance.

He should have expected it, he supposed, with Leo.

His son.

Though his own parents had never indicated they felt anything for Alessandro except mild pleasure if he did well and cold dismissal if he intruded at an inopportune time, he knew what the bond between parent and child should be. When he discovered his son, he'd acted instantly to get custody, desperate to ensure Leo was in the care of a loving parent.

Even though Alessandro knew he had everything to learn about how to love.

He'd never expected it would come so easily.

He watched Leo point out the window and babble, talking to both Carys and Bruno, standing protectively beside them. Something warm inside Alessandro's chest expanded and his lips twitched as he watched his boy's animated face.

His boy.

The happiness Leo had brought into Alessandro's life, and the weighty sense of responsibility, were unprecedented.

He wouldn't change them for anything.

His gaze shifted to Carys and the way her gentle smile lit her face. She did things to him he didn't understand.

A lifetime's lessons in the ways of women had taught him he'd be a fool to give any woman his heart on a platter.

And yet, these past weeks he'd grown...comfortable with

her. Never comfortable enough to ignore the effervescent bubble of lust that was now a constant in his life. But relaxed as he'd never been with any other woman.

So relaxed he had to force himself to remember that, like the rest of her sex, she wasn't above cheating on a man.

Yet looking at her now, so thrilled that he'd given in to her request to do something 'normal' like spend the afternoon sightseeing around the lake, without a limo or a Lamborghini or any other of his 'rich man's toys', he found it hard to believe she could be selfishly calculating.

He didn't want to believe it. That was the most astonishing of all.

He found himself trusting her in so many ways. *Liking* her. Not merely desiring her.

She *was* different.

Her disinterest in cash was genuine. She really did prefer a picnic by the lake to the ostentation of Milan's top restaurants. And though she now spent money from her account, it was mainly on toys and books for Leo rather than fashion for herself.

She was completely different to his mother, who'd had barely a maternal bone in her body. Carys was a wonderful mother.

Alessandro realised his insurance policy, the prenup that provided her with a fortune if she stayed with Leo, hadn't been necessary. Nothing on this earth would drag Carys from her son. Alessandro approved of her for that alone.

And, he realised, for so many other things.

For her indomitable spirit, conquering what he realised were wounds as old and deep as his. Overcoming dyslexia and the ingrained sense of not measuring up, to get on with her life.

Her intelligence. Her quiet dignity.

Carys was the sort of wife a man could be proud of in many ways. With her warmth and generosity of spirit, he saw her taking her place beside him in the public aspects of his life. Livia had fulfilled the public responsibilities of the Contessa Mattani with panache, but with a cool intolerance for what she termed 'the ordinary people' that made him grit his teeth.

Across the cabin Carys stretched and her sundress grew

taut across her breasts. Predictably his body tightened in a spasm of hunger.

Alessandro thought of their slow, languorous lovemaking this morning, of the wonder in her eyes as he brought her to climax and pumped his life essence inside her.

His gaze dipped to her flat belly and excitement stirred. For all they knew she could even now be carrying another of his children. Raw, primal satisfaction smote him at the idea of watching her grow big with his baby. He'd missed that the first time. But now…they could build a family together and he'd participate in every moment.

'Signor Conte.'

Alessandro dragged himself from his thoughts to focus on the small, grey-haired woman before him.

Some sixth sense made Carys turn and look for Alessandro. He stood not far away, head tilted down as he listened to the rotund woman before him. The intensity of his expression, the stillness of his rangy frame, sent a skitter of prescience up her spine.

The woman looked vaguely familiar.

At her side Bruno also watched the pair, making no move to intervene. Yet something was wrong. She sensed it.

'Bruno, would you please take Leo?' She met the minder's startled gaze as she thrust Leo towards him. Barely waiting to see her son settled, she turned towards Alessandro. The woman leaned in, gripping his arm.

Begging? No, that wouldn't leach the colour from Alessandro's face. The woman tilted her head and finally Carys recognised her: Rosina, who'd been Alessandro's housekeeper when he'd lived in his home in the hills behind the lake.

Rosina had been so friendly and warm. She'd encouraged Carys in her tentative attempts to learn Italian. More, she'd provided comfort in the form of a cup of tea or a plate of fruit and admonishment not to starve herself when Carys felt her relationship with Alessandro shatter around her.

Carys squeezed through the seats, eager to greet her, but more than ever concerned by Alessandro's frozen expression. She regretted now that she'd requested they come by ferry instead of private boat or car.

After being surrounded by servants, getting used to her new life as the Contessa Mattani, and absorbing the overwhelming reality of her role as Alessandro's wife, she'd been eager for a 'normal' day with people who hadn't a clue who she was. Had it been a mistake?

By the time she reached the aisle, Rosina had gone and the ferry was coming in to dock. People rose, ready to stream ashore.

Yet Alessandro stood unmoving, as if riveted to the spot. Fear made her heart thump so hard it seemed to catapult around her chest.

She hadn't wanted to care for him, but somehow he'd deviously wormed his way back into her heart. He pleasured her to within an inch of her sanity, comforted her when she needed it, made her feel…special.

She could no longer pretend she didn't care. *Didn't love.*

Carys swallowed a welling knot of anxiety. 'Alessandro?'

He turned and for a moment it seemed as if he didn't see her. His gaze was blank, inward looking. Then he blinked, focused, and snagged her close, away from the people thronging towards the door.

'Bruno has Leo? Good.' He sounded just the same as ever, but he looked…different.

'What is it, Alessandro?' He met her eyes for a moment before looking away, towards the passengers. Somewhere in that crowd was the woman who'd talked to him so earnestly.

'Come.' He curved his arm around her back and led her to the door. 'It's all right. Leo and Bruno are on their way.'

It wasn't all right; Carys could see the pinched line of his mouth and the deep crease in his forehead.

Yet it wasn't till they were ashore and a waiting car had delivered them to the villa, that Carys got any answers. Alessandro gave a sleepy Leo into his nanny's arms, and as if too edgy to settle indoors, led the way to the private path along the lake. He seemed distracted, forgetting to shorten his long pace so she had to scurry to keep up.

'Please, Alessandro.' The look on his face, as if he'd just seen a ghost, frightened her. 'What's wrong? What did Rosina want?'

He turned then, the expression in his shadowed eyes unreadable. 'You remember her?'

'Of course. She was kind to me.' At a time when Carys had felt lost. 'Does she still work for you?' Carys realised she didn't even know if he'd kept his mountain home.

He shook his head. 'When I went to hospital, the house was shut up. She took the retirement she'd put off and moved away to be near her daughter. When I came out of hospital I settled into the family villa instead.'

Was that wistfulness in his voice? The home he'd built had been so like him, vibrantly unique and attractive. Did he miss it?

'But she said something to you.' Something significant.

Alessandro shrugged, walking ahead as her steps slowed.

'She said it was good to see me again, all recovered. Good to see us,' he added after a moment.

Carys started forward. 'She remembered me?' He nodded. 'What else did she say?' There was more. Shadows darkened Alessandro's face, each line etched as if on a lifeless mask.

'She congratulated us on our wedding. She read about it in the papers.'

'And?' Alessandro was stonewalling. After living with him she knew that much.

Suddenly he stopped and turned. 'She was there the day you left.'

The day Alessandro had told her to go. The day he'd found her, dishevelled from holding Stefano Manzoni at bay, and leapt to the conclusion she'd been fooling with her lover, not fighting off a predator. Alessandro's fury had been instantaneous and all consuming, as if the incident had thrown fuel on a long-smouldering fire.

Carys groped for the balustrade between her and the water as memories she'd tried to forget came rushing back.

'I see.'

'No. You don't.' Something in his voice made her turn. His expression baffled her. 'She said that after you left, I couldn't settle. I paced the house from end to end.'

That didn't surprise her. He'd been in a towering rage, for all that he'd kept it tightly leashed. Even his order to leave had been delivered in a lethally quiet whisper that had cut Carys to the bone and slashed through her last hopes that he could ever love her.

'Twenty minutes later I raced out to the car. Apparently I said I was going to bring you back.'

Carys gasped. Her heart stuttered then eventually took up something like its usual rhythm.

Alessandro had gone after her? He'd wanted her back?

Her eyes opened so wide they stung. Did that mean he'd realised his accusations were baseless? Now her heart pounded like a locomotive and adrenaline pulsed in her blood.

He'd chased after her...

Heat flooded Carys at the thought of him racing to stop her leaving. *Of him realising his mistake.*

'But you didn't go to the station.' She'd waited ages for a train.

'No.' Penetrating green eyes met hers. 'That was when I had the accident, speeding along the road after you.'

Dumbfounded, Carys met his shuttered gaze. Guilt replaced the buoyant surge of elation in her veins and she slumped against the balustrade as shock hit her in the knees.

'Carys!' Strong arms dragged her up against a familiar, hard torso and she shut her eyes, unwilling to face just yet the dislike which surely must be in his face now.

Did he blame her for the accident?

She did. Guilt seeped through her bones. She clutched him close, reliving the horror she'd experienced when she'd heard about his accident. But this was worse. So much worse.

Alessandro widened his stance, wrapping Carys closer to his pounding chest. Fear spiked at her sudden pallor. He told himself it was shock, expected in the circumstances, but that didn't ease his concern. He rubbed a hand down her back, willing warmth back into her trembling, chilled form.

It would be OK, he assured himself.

OK? His world had turned upside down!

You were so much in love, both of you. Of course you went to fetch her back.

The words rang in Alessandro's head, pounding in time with the heavy rush of blood surging through his temples.

No! She had that wrong. Must have.

Yet the words resonated, shocking him with their familiarity. Love? Romantic love?

He tried to reject the notion, as he'd rejected it all his life. But the emotions Carys evoked lodged deep inside and wouldn't be removed.

The fact remained that he'd gone after Carys. He'd been wild-eyed and desperate if his former housekeeper was to be believed. Though clearly she had a romantic disposition. No doubt her memory embroidered the event.

That wasn't important. What mattered was knowing if he'd changed his mind because he'd realised he'd been wrong about Carys, or whether he'd decided he didn't care what she'd done—simply had to have her back.

Either option revealed him as emotional, too strongly affected by his lover to think straight.

He didn't want to believe it.

Yet here he was, tied in knots because of this same woman. Feeling so much because of her. Even now her fresh cinnamon scent tangled in his senses, a heady distraction.

He thought through the few concrete facts he'd pieced together about her infidelity. He'd come home to find Stefano Manzoni, a man he'd never trusted, accelerating recklessly down the driveway. He'd found Carys with her blouse undone, her hair down and a fresh love bite on her neck. She'd admitted meeting Manzoni in town and letting him bring her home. Then she'd tried to deflect Alessandro's anger by accusing him instead of infidelity with Carlotta.

What else had there been that he couldn't recall? Was there any more? Had his accusation been as misguided as her belief he'd planned to marry Carlotta?

That didn't seem believable. Yet honesty made him face the possibility he'd jumped to conclusions.

Had Alessandro subconsciously waited for Carys to prove it was his money that really attracted her? That she would dump him for a man who could give her more once the going got tough? As his mother had left his father years before, hooking up with a man whose bank account made the Mattani wealth at that time look insipid by comparison.

Had Alessandro primed himself to expect Carys' betrayal?

He drew a steadying breath, tightening his hold on her, feeling her rapid heartbeat near his, the way her soft form moulded so perfectly to his.

Reluctantly he faced the truth he'd been avoiding.

Despite those few wisps of memory, the gap in his mind was as real as ever. Intimacy with Carys hadn't restored it. He could no longer kid himself that would happen.

He would never remember that part of his past. Never have his memory as absolute proof about her behaviour. He had only the comments of those, like his housekeeper and Carys, who'd been there.

He had logic.

Above all he had his own gut instinct.

What did they tell him?

Carys felt the heavy thud of Alessandro's heart, strong and steady, against her. The way he held her, as if welded to her, made her heart sing, but couldn't blot out her distress.

'I'm sorry,' she murmured at last, clutching his shirt as if to stop him retreating.

'Pardon?' He stepped back a fraction so her voice wasn't muffled against his chest. Carys only just resisted the impulse to burrow back into him, seeking comfort.

'I'm sorry.' Finally she lifted her face. 'If it weren't for me, you wouldn't have crashed. You wouldn't have…' Even now the thought of him in a coma paralysed her larynx.

'You blame yourself?' He tilted his head.

'Don't you?' She remembered the steady rain that day—that was why she'd accepted a man's offer of a lift rather than waiting for a bus. That and the fact that the evening before she'd seen Alessandro with Carlotta. He'd spent the night in town rather than return home, and Carys had finally grown tired of waiting meekly for him to appear. No wonder she'd been distracted enough to fall into Stefano's clutches.

If only she hadn't been so gullible, so ready to believe Livia's plausible lies.

'Of course I don't. Don't be absurd.' Alessandro's eyes flashed dark fire. 'How could you be to blame? I was the one speeding, and the driver that forced me off the road was on the wrong side. It had nothing to do with you.' His gaze held hers so long Carys felt his certainty pulse through her.

'Don't take that upon your conscience, *tesoro,*' he said more gently and cupped her chin in one warm palm. Her heart squeezed tight at such tenderness. It reminded her of how he'd looked, and sounded, so long ago.

'Carys.' He bent his head and touched his lips to hers. Instantly she melted into him, her body alive with the tingle of magic only Alessandro could create. 'Sweet Carys.'

Kisses, soft yet fervent, covered her cheeks, brow, even her nose. Large hands cupped her head, holding her still. Her heart rose in her mouth. These weren't the caresses of a man desperate to bed her. They weren't about sex. They were about emotion. The sort of emotion she'd nurtured so long.

'Forgive me, Carys?'

The kisses stopped, though he didn't release her. Dazedly Carys opened her eyes. The look on her husband's face stole her breath right away. It would have claimed her heart too, if she hadn't already given that to him.

She blinked. 'What are you talking about?'

He didn't speak immediately and she had the bizarre feeling he was gathering his courage. He, the man who felt no qualms about anything, not billion-dollar deals or handling a hungry media scrum.

He breathed deep, his chest expanding so mightily it brushed hers, sparking inevitable flickers of awareness in every erogenous zone.

'These past years have been hard for you,' he murmured, his voice a suede caress that unravelled the ribbon of tension in her stomach. 'I sent you away, and because of that you were alone through your pregnancy and Leo's birth. Alone bringing up our son and making a home for him.' He paused and squeezed his eyes shut as if in pain.

Carys reached out, sliding her trembling fingers over his shoulders, feeling the tension vibrate within him.

'We survived.'

'I deprived myself of you and Leo.' Alessandro's mouth twisted up in a mirthless smile, and when he opened his eyes they were darker than she'd ever seen them. So dark it felt as if she looked right into his soul.

'I should never have let you go. Never have doubted.'

'Sorry?' His admission struck Carys dumb. She read the remorse in his face, felt the powerful energy hum through his body as if he kept a lid on a force too great to be released. But still she couldn't believe.

Long fingers slid round to cradle her face. His gentle touch set a thousand butterflies dancing inside her. A sense of something precious, something miraculous, filled her.

'I'm to blame, Carys. It's my fault. I should never have accused you of betraying me.'

She looked into his eyes and read emotion there, bare and powerful. Remorse. Guilt. Pain. And hope.

The shock of it, of having him reveal such depth of feelings rocked her on her heels. She clung to his shoulders, trying to marshal stunned thoughts.

'You weren't to know,' she found herself saying tentatively, not even questioning her need to ease his pain. 'After all, I believed Livia when she told me you were getting married.'

He shook his head abruptly. 'You weren't to know Livia had her own agenda. Whereas I…I have no one but myself to blame for leaping to conclusions.'

Carys' heart accelerated. 'Rosina told you on the boat? Told you there was nothing between me and Stefano Manzoni?'

Once more Alessandro shook his head. 'No.'

'But then…?'

'How do I know?' Again that raw, self-deprecating smile.

He reached up and took her hand, slid it from his shoulder, past the spot where his heart thundered, then pressed it down against his abdomen. 'I feel it here. Gut instinct, if you like.' He shrugged, still holding her palm against his belly. 'My sixth sense has been telling me all along that you weren't the woman I thought, but I ignored it.'

His eyes glowed emerald fire that melted the last of her defences.

'Two years ago I was wrapped up in saving the company, fixing the mess my father had left behind. I know that much, at least. Plus I'd decided all women were treacherous. I was probably waiting for you to slip up and prove me right.' He shook his head in obvious self-disgust.

Carys remembered the speed with which he'd put two and two together and made five, assuming infidelity where there was none. It *had* seemed as if he'd been all too ready to believe the worst.

She felt as if she'd whirled into an alternate universe, where nothing made sense. For a crazy instant, as he'd dragged her palm down his chest, she'd thought he was going to say it was his heart dictating this change in him. That he loved her.

Now she battled a queasy sensation of burgeoning hope and fear roiling together inside her.

'I don't understand.'

Alessandro was silent so long her nerves screamed with tension. Eventually he shrugged, a tense movement that only reinforced her awareness of his pain.

'Let's just say I've spent too many years as a target for women interested in acquiring wealth and prestige.'

Carys stared. Was it possible Alessandro thought women threw themselves at him for material things they could get from him? Didn't he understand the pull of a devastatingly sexy, macho man? She'd been a sucker for him the moment she saw him, and she'd known nothing of his wealth or position.

'And earlier…' He paused a moment before continuing. She watched his nostrils flare as if he stole a sustaining breath. 'My mother left when I was five. Dumped my father and went off to become the partner of a man whose fortune and prestige was even greater than his. I never saw her again.'

'Your father kept you apart?' Despite the rift between man and wife, to deprive a son of his mother was—

Alessandro snorted. 'My dear mama wasn't interested in me. She'd palmed me off to nannies from the first. In some ways it wasn't such a blow when she left.'

Despite his tight smile, Carys read the lie in his words. Her heart turned inside out, recognising the ancient scars he hid: the knowledge that his mother hadn't wanted him. How devastating that must have been.

Fellow feeling stirred. She felt his hurt deep in her psyche.

'After that it was a succession of nannies, most of them more interested in snaring a man with a title than looking after his son.' Alessandro didn't hide his bitterness for all that his words were clipped. 'I learned not to trust anyone.'

Carys wanted to soothe away the years of built up pain and distrust. To cradle him in her arms as if he were still that little boy distressed at losing his mother.

'But that's no excuse for my behaviour.'

Alessandro lifted her hand and pressed a kiss on her wrist. Another on her palm. Heat juddered through her and suddenly her need to comfort turned into something else. The familiar electrical current flowed from him to her and back again.

His smouldering eyes held her fast.

'Carys. I can't remember what happened between us. I probably never will. But I understand now that I jumped to conclusions and acted rashly.'

Her pulse leapt at the admission.

'Living with you these past couple of months, I realise I misjudged you. I should never have ended it the way I did.'

Her heart swelled as if it would burst as she read the warmth in his gaze.

'Sandro!' It was what she used to call him. The name she'd kept locked away in her heart for so long. Now it slipped out easily. 'Sandro, I—'

He pressed his index finger to her mouth. The male musk scent of his skin teased her. 'Let me say this first, Carys.'

He drew a deep breath and, stunned, she read hesitancy in his expression. Instinct told her this was serious. Her muscles tightened and she almost stopped breathing.

Was it possible her secret hopes were coming true?

'I never expected to feel like this about any woman. You're honest, direct, caring.' He smiled and the impact scrambled her brain. 'And we're good together. Aren't we?'

He looked so serious as he watched for her reaction, almost vulnerable, despite his innate strength.

Carys nodded carefully, trying to remain calm as a high-octane mix of excitement, love and desire ignited inside.

She tugged his hand from her mouth and squeezed it, willing him to say the words she'd waited so long to hear. The words she wanted to share with him.

I love you.

His face was sober as he pulled her close.

'I…trust you, Carys.'

CHAPTER FOURTEEN

'DID you hear me, Carys?' Carlotta tilted her head to one side, looking like an inquisitive little bird.

'Of course I heard.' Carys mustered a smile for her friend, trying to drag her mind back to the conversation.

She spent too much time fretting over what couldn't be changed. Life with Alessandro was good. More than good. He was a great father to Leo, a stupendous lover. Even now the memory of his hands and mouth on her body quickened her pulse. He was kind, attentive.

And he trusted her. Her lips twisted, remembering his words and the depths of her disappointment.

He gave her more than he'd given any other woman. All he had to give.

It wasn't Alessandro's fault he'd never learned what love was. That he couldn't offer it to her.

She would learn, one day, to be content. It didn't matter that she'd craved love all her life. Or that she bestowed it on him unstintingly. She was thankful for what she had, and soon she'd stop wishing for the moon.

The best way to do that was to keep herself busy, as she had these past couple of months.

'Yes, the tutor is terrific. I'm so glad I took your advice about hiring him.' This time her smile was more convincing. If she was going to live here, she had to master the language, which was why she and Carlotta spoke Italian when they were alone. 'I'm improving, don't you think?'

'You're a marvel,' Carlotta said with a smile. 'Your pronunciation is great, even if your vocab has a way to go. You'll be a hit when Alessandro starts entertaining on a large scale again. With that cute hint of an accent everyone will find you enchanting.'

'You think?' Carys glanced around the exclusive hotel restaurant Carlotta had chosen for lunch. Despite her new clothes and her determination to fit into Alessandro's life, she felt a ripple of unease sometimes, as if she didn't belong and everyone knew it.

The fact that Alessandro seemed to keep her apart from the demands of his social schedule didn't help either. Yes, they went out, even had friends to dine occasionally, but it was obvious he turned down a lot of invitations he would normally accept. Because he wasn't sure she'd cope?

'I *know,* Carys. According to the grapevine, the young *contessa* is charming, refreshing and beautifully dressed.' Carlotta laughed. It was she who'd steered Carys through the acquisition of a new wardrobe.

Carys smiled. 'You can take a lot of credit there.'

'Don't be so modest. Now, tell me, how are you going with your speech for the annual charity lunch? Any ideas?'

Carys nodded. 'A few.' In truth, she'd been thinking of little else since she'd heard about it. Each year the Contessa Mattani hosted a charity luncheon in the ballroom of the Mattani villa. Proceeds, along with a sizeable donation from Mattani Enterprises, went to a charity of her choosing, a different one each year. It was a tradition dating back to the time of Alessandro's grandmother.

Now it was a major event on the calendar of Italy's social elite. Anxiety skipped down her spine as she thought of hosting it and delivering a speech to a throng of the country's rich and famous.

'You *will* be there, won't you?'

'I wouldn't miss it for the world. And you'll have Alessandro by your side too.'

Alessandro hadn't spoken to her about it yet. Instead she'd learned about it from Carlotta, then had the date confirmed by the housekeeper. Tonight she'd finally remember to ask him for more details. She'd been meaning to for weeks, but somehow she often found herself…distracted around him.

Carlotta signalled for the bill. 'I'm afraid I have to rush off. Special meeting with a special client.'

'Then you go and I'll pay.'

'Sure?'

'Of course. Don't be late. I'll just sit here a little longer.' Because it was back again, that slight queasiness she'd experienced on and off lately.

'*Ciao, bella.*' Carlotta kissed her on both cheeks. 'I'll call when I'm back from Paris.'

Carys said goodbye and sat back, willing her stomach to settle. She paid the bill, sipping water, trying to stifle excitement that rose even stronger than the nausea.

She'd only felt like this once before. When she'd been pregnant with Leo. Her breasts were tender too. Or was that from Alessandro's thorough loving last night?

A ripple of pleasure tingled through her as she remembered their passion. And at the possibility she could no longer ignore. *Was she pregnant?*

A brother or sister for Leo. Another child to love and cherish. Only this time with Alessandro at her side from the start. Would he be happy? They hadn't taken precautions, so presumably he wasn't averse to the idea.

Surreptitiously she rubbed her palm over her stomach, wonder growing at the possibility.

Eventually she pushed her chair back and made for the foyer, only to falter as she saw a group of well-dressed older women in a group ahead of her.

A familiar voice spoke; a familiar elegantly tall figure blocked her path.

'Of course, I expected it. Poor Alessandro, what choice did he have? The girl was the mother of his child. But now he's stuck with the consequences.' A shrug of bony shoulders emphasised the point.

Carys put her hand to the door jamb, clinging tight as nausea hit again, stronger this time, preventing her from turning and walking away. Besides, her feet were welded to the spot by the scalding venom in Livia's voice.

'She has no breeding, no class, no idea of how to go on. How she's going to fill her responsibilities as *contessa* I can't imagine. Thank goodness I'm in the country for the day of the gala charity luncheon.' She shook her head. 'He asked me to step in and host it. Begged me. I couldn't let him down. We both know his wife would make a hash of it, and the Mattani name is too important to be made a laughing stock.'

Carys didn't hear any more vitriol. She'd finally unlocked her feet and prised her hand from the wall.

'Since the family name is so important to you, I'm surprised to hear you doing your best to taint it.'

Despite the bile rising in her throat, Carys somehow managed to sound cool and in control. Each word emerged with a crystal-clear diction that would have made her language tutor proud.

Amazing what shock and fury could produce. Especially since Carys wanted only to retreat and give in to the nausea.

Instead she stood straighter in her heels and smoke-blue suit of finest local silk. She told herself she looked elegant, even chic, like the countess she now was.

Livia spun round, hectic colour rimming her artfully made-up cheeks.

Carys looked up at the woman who'd tried to destroy what Alessandro and she had shared. For the first time she saw beyond the careful grooming and exquisite sophistication to the ugly greed and discontent beneath.

'Anyone would think you had an axe to grind,' Carys said softly and heard a collective intake of breath from the women watching so avidly. 'That you had your nose put out of joint because you'd been supplanted by Alessandro's wife.' She let a pause lengthen. 'Supplanted by a younger woman.'

The widening of Livia's eyes and a single muffled laugh from the group told Carys she was right.

She was tempted to confront Livia with her lies and machinations. But she refused to play her game and feed gossip to the curious. Instead she summoned a stiff-lipped smile. 'But we know that's nonsense, don't we?'

Livia opened her mouth then shut it, nodding abruptly.

'As for my charity lunch,' Carys continued, 'no doubt there was some misunderstanding about the arrangements. I'll ensure it's sorted and send you an invitation, Livia. I hope your friends will all attend too.'

Dimly she was aware of nods and agreement, but her focus was on the woman before her, who suddenly looked smaller and less assured. Carys didn't feel satisfaction or triumph, just a cold lump of distress in the pit of her belly.

'I must go, but I'll talk to Alessandro about having you to the villa for a meal soon. *Ciao,* Livia.' She pressed obligatory kisses to the other woman's cheeks, heard her automatic responses, then turned and concentrated on putting one foot in front of the other all the way to the entrance.

By the time she was alone in the back of the limo, her rigid control had cracked. She was shaking, her skin clammy, and her stomach heaved anew.

She tried to concentrate on the shock and defeat in Livia's eyes but instead remembered only her words.

What choice did he have? His wife would make a hash of it…he begged me…

No, Carys didn't believe it. Alessandro wouldn't do that to her. Livia had lied again. Carys wouldn't trust her as far as she could lift Alessandro's favourite Lamborghini. As soon as the shaking passed, she'd ring him and he'd confirm it.

He'd told her he trusted her.

He'd looked so sincere she'd believed him without hesitation.

But now that old doubting voice whispered again in her head. Had he said it just to woo her into compliance? To make things easier between them? Pain lanced her chest.

No! He'd meant every word.

Yet maybe trust came in different forms. He might trust her word but not think she was fit for the role of wife to a mega-wealthy industrialist.

Who could blame him?

She hadn't grown up in his world. Didn't know all the rules. And maybe—the thought sneaked up out of nowhere—he secretly believed, as others had, that her reading problems reflected on her capacity in other things.

Another surge of nausea made her hunch in her seat. She spent the next few wretched minutes riding wave after wave of pain, trying to blot out the voice of doubt.

Finally, she sat up straight, staring blind-eyed out the window. The roiling in her stomach was vanquished for now, yet she trembled in the aftermath of distress.

She lifted her chin. No matter that a craven part of her was tempted to agree with Livia, that she didn't know how to go on in these rarefied social circles. Carys was here to stay. She was Alessandro Mattani's wife and she'd prove to everyone, herself included, that she could handle whatever that entailed. She owed it to herself, and to Leo.

Her hand slid to her stomach. If she was going to bring up her family in this place, she couldn't afford to let herself sink into the shadows as she'd done when she was young. She knew what that was like, and it was a place she didn't want to visit again.

She'd worked all her adult life to make something of herself, prove to herself that she was as good as everyone else, and not live down to her family's expectations. She refused to let anyone put her in that position again.

She was tired of being made to feel second best. Even by herself.

Carys slipped her cellphone from her handbag and punched in the number for Alessandro's office. She ignored the tingle of fear running through her. Instead she reminded herself Alessandro trusted her.

Alessandro was out of his car and loping up the front steps before the echo of the Lamborghini's engine died. The front door swung silently open before he reached it.

'Where's my wife?'

Paulo moved back to let him enter. 'I believe madam is still at the pool. Master Leo has had his swim and gone up for a nap.'

'Good.' What needed saying was better done in private. Alessandro strode towards the fitness wing, his sense of urgency growing with each step.

He'd been driving home when his efficient new assistant called, explaining that the *contessa* had rung to ask about arrangements for the charity lunch. When she'd checked, it was to find the fool of a woman who'd been his temporary PA had arranged for Livia to host the event. Despite his express instructions that his step-mother no longer be invited to represent the family or his company.

He speared a hand through his hair, frustration rising. At Livia. At incompetent temps. At himself for not double-checking.

He stalked down the corridor. All the while his assistant's voice echoed in his head. 'No, she didn't leave a message. No, she didn't say anything. She hung up after I told her about the luncheon.'

Alessandro had a bad feeling about this. He knew Carys sometimes felt unsure of herself. That was why he'd taken it slowly introducing her to society. He guessed at the scars her family's treatment of her had caused. Scars he suspected had never truly healed.

He thrust open the door to the pool, shrugging out of his jacket and tie as the warmth hit him. He dropped them on a chair, eyes fixed on the small form swimming in the pool. Usually she swam gracefully. This time there was a dogged determination about her freestyle stroke that spoke more of churning emotion than the need for exercise.

Carys let her palm slam onto the tiles at the end of the pool. She was too tired to make a proper racing turn. Her chest heaved, but still the hurt and anger bubbled inside. She'd do a few more laps, till her mind cleared.

A shadow fell on the tiles. Hands reached down.

'Let me help you out.'

Automatically she kicked out off the wall, propelling herself away. But Alessandro forestalled her by grasping her upper arms and using his extraordinary strength to haul her out to stand before him.

She didn't want to talk to him yet. Not till she was calm. Not till she'd got over the sense of betrayal. It was just a lunch, for goodness sake. Nothing to get worked up about.

Yet it felt like more. Like once again she hadn't measured up.

Like last time when he'd kept her to himself rather than trust her to socialise with his friends. Like all the times her parents hadn't showed, or hadn't remembered or just weren't interested. Like she was doomed to be second best still.

'Look at me, Carys.'

She looked. He stood in a puddle as water sluiced off her body. His trousers were wet from where he'd lifted her, and his shirt clung in a way that made her want to run needy hands over his sculpted chest and torso. The knowledge fuelled her anger just as she was aiming for calm.

'You're home early.' It emerged as an accusation, belying the rapture she'd found so often when he returned in time to play with Leo, then take his wife to bed for some late afternoon loving. She bit her lip and looked over his shoulder.

A finger at her chin inexorably lifted her face towards his. There was no escaping his dark gaze or the sympathy she read there.

She didn't want his sympathy! She wanted so much more.

The futility of it hit her. She'd married Alessandro pretending not to care for him, but she'd known, deep in her heart, that she was fated to love this man no matter how unequal their circumstances or the feelings between them.

Alessandro's heart jammed against his ribs, almost stopped beating, as he saw her reddened eyes.

His indomitable Carys had been crying. The realisation gutted him. His hold on her tightened, but he resisted the need to pull her close. The set of her jaw and the flash of her ice-bright eyes were pure warning.

'I can explain—'

'I'm sure you can.' Bitterness laced her words. 'I suppose your office warned you I'd rung. That I knew you'd asked Livia to take my place.'

'It wasn't like that.' Not in the way she thought. His hands gentled on her shoulders, sliding down her slick arms in an instinctive gesture of comfort.

'Wasn't it?' Her gaze shifted. She didn't want to look at him. 'You think I'm not up to playing the role of *contessa*.'

'Don't say that!' He hated it when she talked of playing a role. As if at any moment she might decide she was tired of the act and simply leave. His fingers tightened and he planted his feet wider, instinctively ready to fight for what was his.

'So you asked Livia, *begged* her to step in.'

'That was a mistake, Carys.'

'You can say that again!' She tried to shrug out of his grip, but he refused to release her. He watched temper war with pain as her lips trembled and her eyes glowed bright with slow burning anger. He wanted to fold her close and soothe her.

'I'm you're *wife*, Alessandro. Not some employee you can put aside if you think they're not up to a job.' The words poured out in a rush. 'You *manipulated* me into this marriage. Gave me no choice in the matter. It's too late to decide now that you didn't get a good bargain when you married me.'

'Now hold on.' She'd hit on a sore spot. He knew a sneaking guilt that he'd forced her into marriage. That he'd taken unfair advantage of a woman who hadn't the resources to withstand him. He'd been utterly ruthless in getting this woman into his home and his bed.

'No, I won't hold on!' She straightened, glaring at him with something akin to hatred in her eyes. That look set his heart pounding and fear skimming through him. A fear such as he'd never known.

He couldn't lose Carys. It was impossible. Not now.

'I'm not some prop to be pulled out and shown to the public when you want a compliant wife, then shoved aside when you think I'm not up to dealing with your aristocratic friends.'

'You can't believe that's what I've been doing!' Indignation warred with sympathy. 'I've been giving you time to adjust, trying not to overwhelm you. I know this is different to what you're used to.'

She wasn't listening, just shook her head and planted her hands dead centre on his chest, pushing as if to make him move away.

He stayed planted exactly where he was. No one, not even Carys, dismissed him.

'I'm tired of this, Alessandro. Tired of being treated as second best. Tired of settling for less.'

'Settling?' His brow knotted. 'What do you mean settling?'

'This *convenient* arrangement of ours,' she said, distaste dripping from every syllable. 'It can't go on like this. I can't—'

'Convenient?' Alessandro tried to obliterate burgeoning panic, funnelling his fears instead into the wrath that surfaced when she spoke of ending their marriage. 'You accused me of that the night we got married, didn't you? You were wrong then and you're wrong now.' After all this time they were back where they'd started. Why couldn't she see how important this was? How important *they* were. 'You think this marriage is *convenient* for me?'

Azure eyes met his, unblinking. Her gaze pierced him to the soul. 'I think you got what you wanted, Alessandro. But it's not enough for me. I—'

He refused to listen to Carys request a divorce. Feelings, more tumultuous than he'd ever experienced, exploded within him, shattering the last of his iron-clad control, leaving him defenceless against the pain that ripped him apart.

'You think *this* is convenient, Carys?' He swooped down and took her mouth with his. The kiss was hard, demanding, proprietorial, almost brutal, but he could no longer hold himself in check.

She was *his*. Absolutely incontrovertibly *his*. Nothing had ever felt as right as holding Carys, kissing her. He pulled her close, enfolded her in an embrace that nothing could break.

He needed her. Wouldn't be whole without her.

The feel of her there, her heart hammering in time with his, her soft lips yielding, even giving back kiss for furious kiss, only strengthened his certainty.

'Or this?' He drew back enough to lick a line from her collarbone to her ear, feeling her judder in response, her breath catch in a gasp of pure pleasure.

'There's nothing convenient about what I feel for you, Carys.' He drew back just enough to hold her dazed eyes with his. 'I refuse to give up the woman I love. Do you hear me? There will be no talk of divorce. I won't accept it. I won't give you up.'

This time when he kissed her, he lifted her right off the ground, securing her with one arm around her bottom, the other around her torso, pulling her to him as if he could meld her wet form into his own.

They were one, damn it. They belonged together.

'Sandro?'

'No.' The coward in him didn't want to hear her pleas to be released from their marriage. Instead he kissed her again, turning and walking the few paces till he felt the wall against his arm. He held her there, secure in his arms, her back to the wall, unable to escape, as he concentrated on ravaging her senses with all the passion welling inside him.

He could swear she responded as ardently as ever. More so. Perhaps, after all, she could be persuaded.

'Sandro.' Only lack of oxygen, the need to breathe again, allowed her to speak.

Her fingers against his lips stopped him when he would have kissed her again to stop the flow of words he didn't want to hear.

'Please, Sandro.' Such emotion in her husky voice. His heart squeezed in sheer terror as he knew he couldn't put off the moment any longer. He drew back enough to look down into her face. But he didn't relinquish his hold. He held her clamped hard against him.

'You love me?' There was wonder in her eyes, and doubt.

He was a proud man. From childhood he'd learned not to share himself, not to trust his heart to anyone else. But what he felt was too big to be hidden.

'Can you doubt it, Carys?' He lifted his hand to stroke her brow, her cheek, her swollen lips. 'I think I loved you even before I saw your picture in that brochure. Definitely from the moment I held you in my arms in my hotel suite, and almost died from the sheer ecstasy of you there, with me.' He swallowed a rising lump in his throat.

'And when I saw you holding our son…' This time his kiss was tender, soft and fleeting. Reluctantly he pulled back, watching her eyes widen.

'I didn't know what love was till I met you, *tesoro mio*. But now I do. It's the glorious warmth I feel just thinking about you. Just remembering your smile when you're not there. It's the desire to keep you safe, to protect you and care for you every day of the rest of our lives. To share my life with you. It would kill me if you left.'

His heartbeat slowed to a sombre, waiting pulse. 'I was only half alive before I found you again. Please…' He didn't care that he laid his innermost self open and vulnerable before her. All that mattered was having Carys in his life.

'Oh, Sandro!' Her kiss was fervent but almost clumsy as she pressed her lips feverishly to his. He felt hot tears slide down his cheek and realised she was crying in earnest.

Guilt scorched him. Did he really want to trap her with sympathy?

'Sandro.' She pressed kisses to his chin, his lips, his face. 'I love you so much. I've always loved you. I thought you'd never feel the same.'

He shuddered with the shock of it. But lifting his head, he saw the truth in her eyes. She glowed incandescently as if lit from within. Even then he couldn't believe.

'But you wanted to leave me. You said so.'

Her smile, through drenched eyes and a tear-stained face, was the most beautiful thing he'd ever seen.

'No. I couldn't do that. Ever.' The words sank into his soul and settled there. A tentative sense of peace washed through him. He lowered his head to kiss her again, but she stopped him.

'I'm here for good, Sandro. I just meant I couldn't put up with accepting less than a real marriage with real responsibilities. I couldn't bear thinking you were ashamed of me, that I wasn't good enough to be your *contessa*.'

'Never say that, *piccolina*.' He hitched her higher so they were at eye level. 'You are the perfect wife for me. In every way.' He let the words echo around the tiled walls, satisfaction filling him.

'The luncheon arrangements were a mistake. I didn't invite Livia to take your place. I—'

Her lips against his stopped his words. Stopped thought. She kissed him with all the sweet pleasure and tenderness love could bestow. Alessandro felt it seep into his very bones. He cradled her close and gave back what she offered so unstintingly.

He loved this woman. Would love her till his dying day. The knowledge was glorious, terrifying and wonderful.

When eventually they pulled apart a fraction, she whispered, 'Tell me later. Much later.'

'But it's important for you to understand.'

She smiled and his heart stopped.

'And I will, Sandro.' Alessandro felt his pulse start again, rocketing into life. 'But it can wait. Nothing is more important than this.' She cupped his face in her hands and gazed into his eyes. 'I love you Alessandro Leonardo Daniele Mattani. We're going to be so happy together.'

CHAPTER FIFTEEN

'ONCE again, thank you all for your generosity.' Carys looked across the crowded ballroom, acknowledging smiles from her audience. Relief sighed through her.

Far from being an unresponsive group, those attending the lunch had embraced her and her chosen charities with disarming enthusiasm.

'And please, when you've finished your meal, feel free to come outside and enjoy the fair.'

At a nod from her, the light curtains covering the series of French doors were pushed aside and the doors flung open.

On the afternoon breeze, children's laughter mingled with the sound of music. A fairground had been set up on the lawns and those who would be the recipients of today's fundraising were enjoying themselves: children. Some from orphanages, some with disabilities and others recuperating from serious illnesses.

Carys stepped down from the small podium, acknowledging applause from all sides.

Her gaze kept straying to the tall figure at the back of the room. His nod and smile confirmed what she saw herself. That the lunch and the speech she'd sweated over so long had been successful.

She guessed he was proud of her. But it was the love in his eyes, clear even from here, that warmed her to the core.

Walking between the tables took for ever as she stopped to talk to those she knew and others eager to introduce themselves.

By the time she reached Sandro, Carys felt as if she'd shaken hundreds of hands, answered thousands of questions. And she revelled in it. The guests' support of the charities she'd chosen touched her heart.

'You're a natural,' said a warm voice as she left the final table.

She stopped, looking up into familiar hooded eyes alive with approval. Sandro took her hand and raised it to his lips. Inevitably she shivered in response and he smiled, recognising the effect he had on her.

'You made them laugh and even made them cry,' he added. 'I've never seen such unabashed enthusiasm for our fundraising before.'

Carys looked at Leo, bright-eyed and excited, on his father's hip. Her heart swelled seeing him so happy. Feeling the bond between the three of them.

She shrugged. 'A lot of them are parents. Besides, who wouldn't want to help those kids and make life a little easier for them?'

Alessandro gathered her close with his free arm and she went willingly, content to be in her husband's strong embrace. Content, at last, to be home.

'The hotel industry lost a treasure when you left,' he murmured. 'But I'm not giving you back. You make the perfect Contessa Mattani.' His voice dropped to a low purr. 'You're perfect for me, *piccolina*.' He lowered his head.

'Sandro,' she hissed. 'We can't! Not here.'

His response was to kiss her till her bones tingled and she clung to him.

Some time later she became aware of Leo leaning in for a hug, and sound swelling around them. The sound of laughter and more applause.

Alessandro looked over her head and waved to their guests, then led her out into the gardens.

'We can't just leave them,' she protested.

'Of course we can,' he assured her. 'Today is a treat for the local children.' His gaze dropped to her still-flat stomach, and he smiled, a secret, possessive smile that turned her limbs to jelly.

'Let's give ours a treat too, before we sneak away for a

weekend at our place in the mountains.' He hitched Leo higher and drew Carys further into the balmy afternoon.

She went willingly, knowing there was nowhere else on earth she'd rather be.

* * * * *

*Harlequin Intrigue top author Delores Fossen presents
a brand-new series of breathtaking romantic suspense!*
TEXAS MATERNITY: HOSTAGES
The first installment available May 2010:
THE BABY'S GUARDIAN

Shaw cursed and hooked his arm around Sabrina.

Despite the urgency that the deadly gunfire created, he tried to be careful with her, and he took the brunt of the fall when he pulled her to the ground. His shoulder hit hard, but he held on tight to his gun so that it wouldn't be jarred from his hand.

Shaw didn't stop there. He crawled over Sabrina, sheltering her pregnant belly with his body, and he came up ready to return fire.

This was obviously a situation he'd wanted to avoid at all cost. He didn't want his baby in the middle of a fight with these armed fugitives, but when they fired that shot, they'd left him no choice. Now, the trick was to get Sabrina safely out of there.

"Get down," someone on the SWAT team yelled from the roof of the adjacent building.

Shaw did. He dropped lower, covering Sabrina as best he could.

There was another shot, but this one came from a rifleman on the SWAT team. Shaw didn't look up, but he heard the sound of glass being blown apart.

The shots continued, all coming from his men, which meant it might be time to try to get Sabrina to better cover. Shaw glanced at the front of the building.

So that Sabrina's pregnant belly wouldn't be smashed against the ground, Shaw eased off her and moved her to a sitting position so that her back was against the brick wall. They were close. Too close. And face-to-face.

He found himself staring right into those sea-green eyes.

How will Shaw get Sabrina out?
Follow the daring rescue and the heartbreaking
aftermath in THE BABY'S GUARDIAN
by Delores Fossen,
available May 2010
from Harlequin Intrigue.

Copyright © 2010 by Delores Fossen

HARLEQUIN® *Blaze*™

is proud to introduce...

New York Times **bestselling author**

Brenda Jackson

with
SPONTANEOUS

Kim Cannon and Duan Jeffries have a great thing going. Whenever they meet up, the passion between them is hot, intense…spontaneous. And things really heat up when Duan agrees to accompany her to her mother's wedding. Too bad there's something he's not telling her.…

Don't miss the fireworks!

Available in May 2010
wherever Harlequin Blaze books are sold.

---

red-hot reads

www.eHarlequin.com

HB79542

Bestselling Harlequin Presents® author

Lynne Graham

introduces

VIRGIN ON HER WEDDING NIGHT

Valente Lorenzatto never forgave Caroline Hales's abandonment of him at the altar. But now he's made millions and claimed his aristocratic Venetian birthright—and he's poised to get his revenge. He'll ruin Caroline's family by buying out their company and throwing them out of their mansion... unless she agrees to give him the wedding night she denied him five years ago....

**Available May 2010
from Harlequin Presents!**

www.eHarlequin.com

HP12915

HARLEQUIN® *Blaze*™

is proud to present

New York Times bestselling author

Vicki Lewis Thompson

with a brand-new trilogy,
SONS OF CHANCE
where three sexy brothers
meet three irresistible women.

Look for the first book
WANTED!

Available beginning in June 2010
wherever books are sold.

---

red-hot reads

www.eHarlequin.com

HB79548

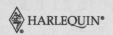

HARLEQUIN®

INTRIGUE®

BESTSELLING
HARLEQUIN INTRIGUE® AUTHOR

DELORES
FOSSEN

PRESENTS AN ALL-NEW
THRILLING TRILOGY

TEXAS MATERNITY:
HOSTAGES

When masked gunmen take over the maternity ward
at a San Antonio hospital, local cops, FBI and the scared
mothers can't figure out any possible motive. Before
long, secrets are revealed, and a city that has been on
edge since the siege began learns the truth behind the
negotiations and must deal with the fallout.

LOOK FOR

THE BABY'S GUARDIAN, May
DEVASTATING DADDY, June
THE MOMMY MYSTERY, July

www.eHarlequin.com

HI69472

LARGER-PRINT
BOOKS!

HARLEQUIN *Presents*~

GET 2 FREE LARGER-PRINT
NOVELS PLUS 2 FREE GIFTS!

YES! Please send me 2 FREE LARGER-PRINT Harlequin Presents® novels and my 2 FREE gifts (gifts are worth about $10). After receiving them, if I don't wish to receive any more books, I can return the shipping statement marked "cancel". If I don't cancel, I will receive 6 brand-new novels every month and be billed just $4.55 per book in the U.S. or $5.24 per book in Canada. That's a saving of at least 13% off the cover price! It's quite a bargain! Shipping and handling is just 50¢ per book.* I understand that accepting the 2 free books and gifts places me under no obligation to buy anything. I can always return a shipment and cancel at any time. Even if I never buy another book, the two free books and gifts are mine to keep forever.

176/376 HDN E5NG

Name	(PLEASE PRINT)	
Address		Apt. #
City	State/Prov.	Zip/Postal Code

Signature (if under 18, a parent or guardian must sign)

Mail to the Harlequin Reader Service:
IN U.S.A.: P.O. Box 1867, Buffalo, NY 14240-1867
IN CANADA: P.O. Box 609, Fort Erie, Ontario L2A 5X3

Not valid for current subscribers to Harlequin Presents Larger-Print books.

**Are you a subscriber to Harlequin Presents books
and want to receive the larger-print edition?
Call 1-800-873-8635 today!**

* Terms and prices subject to change without notice. Prices do not include applicable taxes. Sales tax applicable in N.Y. Canadian residents will be charged applicable provincial taxes and GST. Offer not valid in Quebec. This offer is limited to one order per household. All orders subject to approval. Credit or debit balances in a customer's account(s) may be offset by any other outstanding balance owed by or to the customer. Please allow 4 to 6 weeks for delivery. Offer available while quantities last.

Your Privacy: Harlequin Books is committed to protecting your privacy. Our Privacy Policy is available online at www.eHarlequin.com or upon request from the Reader Service. From time to time we make our lists of customers available to reputable third parties who may have a product or service of interest to you. If you would prefer we not share your name and address, please check here. ☐

Help us get it right—We strive for accurate, respectful and relevant communications. To clarify or modify your communication preferences, visit us at www.ReaderService.com/consumerschoice.

HPLP10R

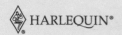
HARLEQUIN®

Showcase

On sale May 11, 2010

Reader favorites from the most talented voices in romance

Save $1.00 on the purchase of 1 or more Harlequin® Showcase books.

SAVE $1.00

on the purchase of 1 or more Harlequin® Showcase books.

Coupon expires Oct 31, 2010. Redeemable at participating retail outlets.
Limit one coupon per purchase. Valid in the U.S.A. and Canada only.

52609015

Canadian Retailers: Harlequin Enterprises Limited will pay the face value of this coupon plus 10.25¢ if submitted by customer for this product only. Any other use constitutes fraud. Coupon is nonassignable. Void if taxed, prohibited or restricted by law. Consumer must pay any government taxes. Void if copied. Nielsen Clearing House ("NCH") customers submit coupons and proof of sales to Harlequin Enterprises Limited, P.O. Box 3000, Saint John, NB E2L 4L3, Canada. Non-NCH retailer—for reimbursement submit coupons and proof of sales directly to Harlequin Enterprises Limited, Retail Marketing Department, 225 Duncan Mill Rd., Don Mills, ON M3B 3K9, Canada.

U.S. Retailers: Harlequin Enterprises Limited will pay the face value of this coupon plus 8¢ if submitted by customer for this product only. Any other use constitutes fraud. Coupon is nonassignable. Void if taxed, prohibited or restricted by law. Consumer must pay any government taxes. Void if copied. For reimbursement submit coupons and proof of sales directly to Harlequin Enterprises Limited, P.O. Box 880478, El Paso, TX 88588-0478, U.S.A. Cash value 1/100 cents.

5 65373 00076 2   (8100)0 11651

® and TM are trademarks owned and used by the trademark owner and/or its licensee.
© 2009 Harlequin Enterprises Limited   HSCCOUP0410

HARLEQUIN *Presents*

Coming Next Month

in **Harlequin Presents**®. Available April 27, 2010:

#2915 VIRGIN ON HER WEDDING NIGHT
Lynne Graham

#2916 TAMED: THE BARBARIAN KING
Jennie Lucas
Dark-Hearted Desert Men

#2917 BLACKWOLF'S REDEMPTION
Sandra Marton
Men Without Mercy

#2918 THE PRINCE'S CHAMBERMAID
Sharon Kendrick
At His Service

#2919 MISTRESS: PREGNANT BY THE SPANISH BILLIONAIRE
Kim Lawrence

#2920 RUTHLESS RUSSIAN, LOST INNOCENCE
Chantelle Shaw

Coming Next Month

in **Harlequin Presents**® EXTRA. Available May 11, 2010.

#101 THE COSTANZO BABY SECRET
Catherine Spencer
Claiming His Love-Child

#102 HER SECRET, HIS LOVE-CHILD
Tina Duncan
Claiming His Love-Child

#103 HOT BOSS, BOARDROOM MISTRESS
Natalie Anderson
Strictly Business

#104 GOOD GIRL OR GOLD-DIGGER?
Kate Hardy
Strictly Business

HPECNMBPA0410